Praise for *Dry Your Tears to Perfect Your Aim*

"By turns a revolutionary's memoir, an adventurer's journal, autofiction, and speculative fiction, yet *Dry Your Tears to Perfect Your Aim* always stays clear and committed to its searching style, and this makes it a novel for today's uncertain world."
—Kaie Kellough, author of *Dominoes at the Crossroads*

"A stunning thought experiment where our hypocrisy, culpability, and compassion are all exposed, *Dry Your Tears to Perfect Your Aim* is a thought-provoking work of secular expiation, a knowing knot of courage and its opposite, and a defiant work of desperate grace."
—Eugene Lim, author of *Search History*

T0182729

Dry Your Tears to Perfect Your Aim

Jacob Wren

Book*hug Press
Toronto 2024

Library and Archives Canada Cataloguing in Publication
Title: Dry your tears to perfect your aim / Jacob Wren.
Names: Wren, Jacob, author.
Identifiers: Canadiana (print) 20240345703 | Canadiana (ebook) 20240345738
ISBN 9781771669047 (softcover)
ISBN 9781771669054 (EPUB)
Subjects: LCGFT: Novels.
Classification: LCC PS8595.R454 D79 2024 | DDC C813/.54—dc23

The production of this book was made possible through the generous assistance of the Canada Council for the Arts and the Ontario Arts Council. Book*hug Press also acknowledges the support of the Government of Canada through the Canada Book Fund and the Government of Ontario through the Ontario Book Publishing Tax Credit and the Ontario Book Fund.

Book*hug Press acknowledges that the land on which we operate is the traditional territory of many nations, including the Mississaugas of the Credit, the Anishnabeg, the Chippewa, the Haudenosaunee, and the Wendat peoples. We recognize the enduring presence of many diverse First Nations, Inuit, and Métis peoples, and are grateful for the opportunity to meet and work on this territory.

The title of this book is a slight variation on the line "dry your tears to improve your aim," which comes from the poem "The News Vendor," by the Nicaraguan poet Daisy Zamora. I first read it in the book *Risking a Somersault in the Air: Conversations with Nicaraguan Writers*, by Margaret Randall.

Contents

1: My Apologies ... 13

2: Care and Time ... 49

Interlude ... 113

3: Desire Without Expectation ... 117

4: Some Future ... 147

Afterword ... 195

Maybe what's needed is to write with the awareness of being wrong. Can one's wrongness be a source of compassion.
—Kate Zambreno, *Appendix Project*

Not to make yourself stupid from the power of others and not from your own powerlessness.
—Alexander Kluge

1: My Apologies

Dropping bombs is the purest form of capitalism. A Tomahawk missile costs US$1.87 million. An AGM-114 Hellfire costs US$150,000. The price of a GBU-44/B Viper Strike is currently unlisted but is likely also somewhere in this range. And the moment they hit the ground, the moment they detonate, the money is gone and you must buy new ones in order to do it all over again. A computer lasts from three to five years. A car lasts eleven. But a bomb, when you use it, lasts a split second and it's gone. A bomb that kills many and a bomb that kills no one costs the same amount. It is not like throwing good money after bad or watching money burn. It's like watching money detonate, watching money explode, like a Hollywood film in which the many explosions make up for the shortcomings of the script, filling in for absences of meaning and purpose.

The term *planned obsolescence* is generally attributed to the industrial designer Brooks Stevens, who used it as the title of a 1954 talk. Wikipedia says Stevens defined it as "instilling in the buyer the desire to own something a little newer, a little better, a little sooner than is necessary." His view was to always make the consumer want something new, rather than to create poor products that would need replacing. But you do not need to wait for a bomb or missile to wear out or become obsolete, or for a newer, better one to arrive on market. Instead they incinerate themselves as an expression of their use. Profit and obsolescence meld into one indistinguishably violent act.

I'm ashamed I decided to take this trip. The moment I got on the first plane, I already knew it was a mistake. That by simply deciding to take this trip I was more part of the problem I hoped to solve than the solution I hoped to become. I paid taxes in a country that was involved in between seven and nine wars, depending on who you asked. My tax money went to pay for a minuscule fraction of the aforementioned bombs. In each of these seven to nine declared and undeclared wars, hundreds if not thousands of such bombs were detonated every year.

I felt a certain powerlessness—I could only read about these wars, only imagine them, had no idea what they were actually like, what it might feel like to be there, to put one's life on the line. For some reason, despite my severe and often literary depression, I did not have the courage to kill myself. But if a bomb that my tax dollars had a very small part in creating were to fall on me, there might be a strange kind of justice to it, as if something had come full circle. And if not, hopefully I would still learn about a situation that, against every ethical desire I held dear, I still played some small (well, minuscule) part in funding. I look around: almost everyone else is asleep. I've always envied people who could sleep easily on planes, always thought they were less tormented than me. I suppose most people *are* less tormented than me. I do not believe this is a contentious statement.

As I go through customs, they look at my passport, then ask the purpose of my trip. I say, "Tourist." They look skeptical, replying that no one comes to sightsee war. I think: that's probably not even true. I'm sure that every time there's a war, all sorts show up to have a quick look. To risk their lives in search of adventure. But that's not what I say. With no idea whether it is wise or unwise, I spontaneously decide

14

that it is better to lie, so I say that some of my ancestors had lived here, and I wanted to see what it looked like before it was completely destroyed. From the expression on the customs officer's face I cannot tell if he likes this answer, or if he believes me, or if he simply wanted a bribe. I rarely lie, and after I get through, I ask myself long and hard why I had chosen this particular moment to do so. In retrospect, it seems stupid to tell a border official that his hometown will be completely destroyed. And needlessly cruel, ignorant. I now wish I'd said something else.

I have one friend here. (Perhaps another reason for my trip.) She kindly picks me up at the airport. I am exhausted after the long flight. In the car, we drive through bombed-out streets. The amount of destruction is almost breathtaking. I realize I've never seen anything like this and don't know how to react. I stare out the window of the beat-up car. You had to be a complete asshole to come here only because you wanted to see all this for yourself, but I thought it was even worse to ignore it, to pretend it wasn't happening or it didn't exist. I could have come as part of a humanitarian project, to help people, feed them or rebuild their houses, but it hadn't occurred to me until now. In the car we don't talk, I just stare out the window. For no specific reason, I begin to cry.

In her small apartment we begin to make dinner. We haven't seen each other in a long time. She moved back here to look after her ailing parents. Now both her parents are gone, but she has stayed. When I wrote to tell her I was coming, she was obviously surprised, so surprised I might even describe it as shocked. In her reply, she said she remembered me as someone who never travelled except for work. This is still basically true, and yet now I seem to be making an exception. In that same reply she also said something that is now burned into my mind. She said that every single day she thinks of leaving. Of becoming yet another name on the list of an ongoing refugee crisis. That every day she's afraid for her life. But, at the same time, she feels there are things she can do here that are more important than what she can do anywhere else in the world. How she never realized home was home until its daily reality was under threat.

Over dinner we talk about surface things. People we used to know, where they are now, what they are up to. Books we've read, movies we've seen. We're both dying to talk politics but neither of us dares. I don't have many friends. When I was younger I had friends, but so many of them have moved away and I never managed to make new ones. I have stayed in touch with almost everyone who moved, but only in a perfunctory, minimal way. When we see each other we catch up, much like we're doing now. I wonder, if I were to die here, how long it would take anyone to notice. Eventually someone would, but it might be a while. I didn't tell anyone I was doing this. No one knows but me, the border guard, and my old friend sitting at the table across from me.

I try, I do my best, to explain the reasons for my trip, and I can tell right away that she doesn't like it. I knew she wouldn't. She says she's never heard such a stupid example of misguided thinking. I know she's right but also feel there's something she doesn't see. Some reason that I have to do this that neither of us will ever understand. What I'm saying suddenly feels mystical to me, and I've never before thought of myself as mystical. She tells me I should get on a plane and go home, protest against my own government back there, or fight to replace them with something—anything—better. If I want to do something, those are causes worth dedicating your life to. Not come here to experience first-hand the violence almost everyone else she knows would give almost anything to escape. I know she's right. But I feel as helpless at home as I feel here, as unable to change anything about my government as I am to make all wars stop. Knowledge is experiential. I already know what it's like at home. I need to know something else, perhaps feel my life at risk, perhaps even let it go and find out if that changes anything. She's disgusted by my explanations. She tells me it's the most sickeningly apolitical thing she's ever heard. I wonder if I think what I'm doing here is political. It's agitated by political reflections but, if I'm honest with myself, it has more to do with being depressed.

In the morning we have breakfast and continue our disagreement. Over the night a new thought has occurred to her. That I'm not just here to stupidly risk my life and take in the suffering of others—a suffering I feel partly responsible for but also don't know how to stop—but that I'm also hoping to make a book out of it. It is so obvious, she doesn't know why it didn't occur to her before. She tells me, almost as a confession, that she's always liked my books, that she feels I try to write about these questions in complex ways, to write my way out of my own political paralysis. But my books have always been works of pure imagination. I've written about suicide but never put my life at risk, as far as she knows I've never tried to kill myself. I've written about revolutions but never tried to make or join one. Why now? As works of pure imagination, my books were productive and perhaps energizing. But I'm only a tourist here, and no matter how much I observe, I will never get it right. I can't write her experience, much less the experiences of so many here who have it so much worse or who have already been killed or martyred.

However, if there's one thing I truly know in this moment, it's that I'm not here to write about it. I didn't come here to write about the experience. For a brief moment I lost my mind, bought a plane ticket. Because I wanted to see for myself. And now that I'm here I have to go through with it. I remember an interview I read a long time ago with a writer, about their first book, how they said they were writing it in order to "stay alive," to keep despair at bay and in the process save themselves. That is also what writing has most often been for me. But this is something else. I'm not here to write about it. I'm here to experience something first-hand for once in my fucking life. To get something about the world. Something I'm complicit in but have never felt and therefore don't think I really understand. Or, to put it more concisely, tentatively, and against all reason: I have some small hope this experience will change my life. Like going to the casino and betting one's entire life savings on a single number: either you lose everything or you win in some way you're barely even able to imagine.

So often, when I argue, I get nowhere. We both dig in our heels, double down on our positions. I want to listen to her deeply, feel that I'm really listening, let her persuade me, but I already agree with so much of what she's saying. I tell her I understand her position, she laughs and looks at me almost in disgust, and I suggest we put it aside for now and go for a walk. She doesn't reply, but from the way she continues to stare at me I understand that one doesn't simply "go for a walk" here. It is too dangerous. She continues to stare at me, wondering what she could say to change my mind, to knock some sense into me. I ask her if we're still friends and she says that we are. That she'll write about what good friends we used to be when she writes my obituary. I laugh and say I'll go for a walk myself and she shouldn't worry. Then she says that she *is* worried. That she's worried precisely because she's my friend. And that she's never thought of me as a person who knows a lot about friendship, but when you have a friend, you don't want them to die. And you especially don't want them to die stupidly, by strolling into a war zone, in a way that could so easily be avoided. But she can also see that I'm lost, she's always thought of me as lost, but I'm more lost now than back when she knew me. She can see that I'm lost, that I've painted myself into a corner, and there's an Italian expression I'm reminding her of right now: when you're painted into a corner, sometimes the only thing to do is shoot yourself in the foot. She just hopes I shoot myself in the foot and not in the head.

Out on the street, life is muted but goes on. It's true no one seems out for a casual stroll, but people are out on the street regardless, walking briskly, doing the things they have to do, going from place to place. There are even a few children playing, but few enough that I assume other children have been told to stay inside. Some of the people stare at me, I suppose wondering if I'm a soldier in civilian clothes (I assume I don't look much like a soldier), and if I'm not a soldier, what the fuck am I doing here, wandering at a pace considerably more casual than anyone else on the street, a flâneur on streets inhospitable to such activities. A formation of planes flies above, and everyone starts walking a bit faster, heading for cover yet without any real panic, as I stop in my tracks and watch the sky. I know nothing about planes, but these ones don't appear primed to attack, seem to be in transit, off to attack someone else a little farther along. They move smoothly through the serene blue sky, and just then, as I'm watching, one of the planes in the formation explodes. I see no reason for it. There are no shots fired, nothing under attack, nothing but five planes in the air, a ball of flame, a trail of smoke, and then there were four. No one else on the street seems especially interested or perturbed by what we just witnessed—business as usual. They've seen it all and they've seen it all before. But I think, in the distance, I hear a few voices cheer.

When I get back to her apartment I tell my friend about what I saw, about the plane that exploded in mid-air. She doesn't seem particularly interested, instead wants to continue our conversation about what I'm about to do. We argue more, but unlike before, now when we argue we also laugh. I think, while I was on my walk, she decided that if I was going to die we should at least have some good times together before I go.

That night she took me to a secret, illegal art party. I was surprised that she was unsurprised by the warplane I had seen explode. She told me it happens regularly and no one knew what to make of it. I felt there was something exciting about the phenomenon, that it presented possibilities, or at least promising questions, but my friend wasn't so sure.

To get to the party, we drove to a suburb of a suburb. Several times, as we drove, we heard planes overhead, and each time we heard that sound we drove just a little bit faster. We parked by a fence, climbed over it (I ripped my pants as we did so), then walked for a long time, I would guess almost an hour. There was a door with a password, another door with a different password, and then stairs going down and down and down. After such a long journey I was thinking that no party could possibly be good enough to make it worth this endless travel but I was wrong. I had no idea what I was talking about.

On our walk I asked again about the exploding planes. She told me the rumour she had heard was that about one plane was exploding every other day. And strangely, it seemed it was democratic, not only planes from any particular government or army or faction. Planes from all countries appeared to be exploding more or less equally. We talked about whether it could be a computer virus, perhaps a computer virus that had gotten out of hand, spread beyond its original target, or another form of sabotage. My friend didn't discount these possibilities—in fact, she didn't discount any possibilities, any explanation might be possible—but I couldn't help but feel she wasn't particularly interested in the explanation. For her it was happening and that was all, another mad thing in this endless series of madnesses called war and colonization.

"But don't you think it's actually great," I asked her, unable to understand her patient lack of excitement.

"It might be great," she replied, "I don't know. The longer I live here, the more suspicious I become. I don't want to get my hopes up if they'll only be dashed a few days later. And also, the pilots...they might be enemy pilots, they're definitely killing us much more, a lot more indiscriminately, than we're killing them. But I don't know why, I find myself not wanting to rejoice in the deaths of those enemy pilots. I'm afraid of becoming obsessed with revenge. I mean, the longer I live here, the more I'm becoming obsessed with revenge, and therefore the more I try to counterbalance it by not rejoicing in these pilots' deaths."

"I'm not talking about revenge," I say. "I'm talking about curiosity, about wanting to know why."

"The planes are exploding. Whether or not we know why, they're exploding."

I say nothing. I still didn't understand.

Stepping into that party, into the first room, I felt something opening up. A sense of possibility I don't think I'd felt in a very long time. Then I immediately started feeling guilty, as if I was here to experience a meaning I was unable to experience at home but that I was getting without the daily pain that made it possible (though perhaps the pain would come later). I walked into the middle of that first room and froze. Things were happening all around me, I could also hear other things happening in the further rooms, and I still hadn't gotten my bearings. Frozen in the middle of that room, it was as if I split into two, as if one part of me had broken off and floated toward the ceiling with the intention of giving the other part a lecture. The lecture was as follows: Now is not the time to feel guilty or beat yourself up. There will be plenty of time for that later. When you stepped into this room, you had an experience of opening. When was the last time you had an experience of opening? Don't throw that away for a wallow in cheap guilt. Your friend brought you to this party, you don't have a lot of friends, take it in and enjoy it. You might be dead tomorrow and never have another chance. It was a good lecture, good self-advice, and I did my best to listen, though I don't think I entirely succeeded.

On the large walls on either side of me were 35 mm projections. One was a montage of randomly exploding planes, the other footage of wildlife in the bombed-out ruins of the city: a few rabbits, a stray deer, two camels that followed each other like a couple, and another animal I didn't recognize. If I had seen these films at home, I might have thought they were good, more art that I was free to take or leave, but here they were life as it was happening all around us and disappearing. I knew I was being romantic but told myself that perhaps being romantic was part of the opening. Being romantic was the flip side of my stupid guilt. In the next room a choir of young people were reading out an endless list of names in unison. I knew these were the names of people who had died, had been killed, but also I didn't want to know, didn't want to have what I knew confirmed. At home I wouldn't have found this performance good, would have found it too literal and heavy-handed, but here it became something else, a kind of simple necessity to have these names spoken out loud and witnessed. It was performance like I had seen a million times before. Why did I suddenly care about it now? I imagined that I was killed tomorrow, my name being added to the list. But, of course, my name would not be added. They were all local names.

My friend finds me and I tell her I think the names are all people who have been killed and she laughs. They're all names of contemporary artists, filmmakers, and writers, most of whom are still alive. She pauses, listens to about a dozen names, then looks at me, saying that at least those dozen we just heard are all, to the best of her knowledge, still alive, then laughs at me again, how I made the most simplistic and literal assumption. She tells me that for her it feels good to hear these names celebrated, to hear art from her home and from the surrounding countries cele- brated. That it's a nice change from the endless names of war. All through the party—and we stayed all night—it was as if I was being reminded what art was for. Or not even reminded: as if I was learning what art was for, learning again what art could be, as if for the first time. Or at least learning one thing it could be for.

We walked through to the next room together. I couldn't tell how many, but there were doors leading in all directions, and I found myself unsure what this place used to be, some sort of underground labyrinth or bunker. My friend actually didn't know; so far she had known the answer to almost every question I'd asked, but it was the first time she'd been here as well. What she did know was that these parties had been happening every year since the war began, which meant this was the ninth or tenth one. Every time the party happened in a different location and each time it was a bit more elaborate than the last. Everyone wanted to participate and everyone wanted to attend. She knew a few of the organizers, but there were many more she didn't know. She told me that part of her good reputation here derived from the fact that her work had been shown at the very first one, the very first party that almost no one attended, making it borderline legendary, a legend she was happy to have benefited from over the years. She wasn't sure she wanted acclaim, but if acclaim were to accrue from something that was pure luck, purely accidental, being in the right place at the right time, she didn't see any particular harm in it. She said that perhaps she preferred success that came from rumour as opposed to more official success. I wondered if she thought of me as someone who preferred it the other way round, but I didn't ask. She was talking about herself, not about me, and I knew it was better to keep the conversation about her and her work. I have a tendency to talk too much about myself, and even though I wasn't sharing these thoughts, I was thinking too much about myself now and that was almost as bad. I told myself it was almost as bad, but I knew, in fact, it was worse.

We slowly walk toward the next room as I ask her about it, what she showed at that very first party nine or ten years ago. As we walk, it seems that she's thinking, I assume she's thinking how best to describe it, a work she made so long ago. She has already told me that since she came back here, time has changed for her, moving back, and the war has done all sorts of strange things to her sense of time. So has the death of her parents. We come to a room full of large paintings. My first thought is that these are the most apolitical paintings I have ever seen. Which is insane, because like anyone who has seen a large number of paintings in their life, I must have seen thousands of paintings that have absolutely no interest in politics. And why must I view all works of art through my political desires? These were large, nineteenth-century domestic scenes—dinners, walks in the park, hunting, marriages—painted with certain flourishes of abstraction, mainly in dark browns and bright reds. I felt they were apolitical, but as I stared at them longer I could also feel anger in their approach. My friend tells me she recognizes the figures, they are the first generation of colonizers, people her grandparents or great-grandparents might recognize because some of their pictures were on the money. They imposed their values and sent the wealth back home. It was never officially a colony, but it might as well have been. Then socialism in its infancy, then socialism crushed by dictatorships, dictatorships covertly funded by my government, then the dictatorships wanted the wealth for themselves, and now bombs to reopen the markets and whatever national resources come along with such openings. This could be one of so many places, the slightly abstracted figures in these paintings like so many aggressive historical foreigners happy to call such places their own.

"At that first party I played a recording of my parents. On

repeat." As we stared at the paintings I listened to my friend. "I was just realizing they were going to die, I had never actually thought about my parents dying before they wrote to me and asked me to take care of them, and as part of this realization I wanted to record them. It was a time when I wasn't sure if I still thought of myself as an artist, if I was still thinking of myself as an artist. I was doing more community projects, wondering how to make use of my life, if there was a way I could use it more directly to help people. Those were the kinds of things we used to talk about at school." I said I remembered, that I still remembered those conversations, they've stayed with me. "When I recorded my parents, I wasn't thinking it was going to become art. I just wanted to record them. But then I was asked if I had anything to show at the party, and I hadn't actually made art in a long time, all I had was the recordings. My parents weren't talking about anything so interesting, just their lives before the war, how they tried to have a good life, not get arrested, go to work, love each other and their friends, stay out of trouble. I was surprised how many people who came to that first party knew my parents, or had met them, they were still alive then. They were actually more social than I thought, friendly with everyone. And my parents were so happy to be part of my art, even though I barely even thought of myself as an artist anymore. They really took it in the best possible way. They came from a generation with such respect for art and culture. Mainly they preferred more traditional works: paintings and films and novels. But if my work was more modern, more contemporary, they loved me so they were going to love that too. Before they gave their approval, I was worried I might be exploiting them, using their words for my own ends and it might be wrong to do so. But when they died, it was the strangest thing. I knew that one of the last things I had done, one of the last things they saw me do, actually made them happy. Many of the choices I've made in life, they didn't like them so much, they didn't always approve, though they did their best to be supportive. But they were so happy I had used their voices in my art."

I didn't know what to say, so we walked in silence. I thought back to when I used to know her, tried to remember if she had ever said anything about her parents, but nothing like that had stuck in my mind. We walked though several rooms, barely even looking at the art or each other. I said: "That's a really beautiful story." Some others came over to say hello and she introduced me. We got talking and, I'm not sure how it came up, but I told them how I had seen a plane explode and was once again perplexed by how deeply unimpressed they all seemed. It apparently happened all the time, with such frequency it was barely worth mentioning. They were all sure there was some devious and logical explanation for the phenomenon, even if no one yet knew exactly what it was. We continued walking as a now-larger group, it felt like there must have been hundreds of rooms spanning in all directions, and I considered again why I had come here. So often in my life I had done so little and now I was taking this insane trip, of which my current location was probably the most sane part. But I was surrounded by art, and meeting new people, their perspectives so different from my own I could often barely follow the conversation as they switched in and out of my language and we wandered through the rooms and through the art. For that long moment I felt strangely happy. But I also knew the moment would pass.

I had to leave in the middle of the night. I told myself I have to leave in the middle of the night because, if I leave during the day, my friend might try again to convince me not to go and this time she might succeed. I had written her a good-bye note I was going to leave on the kitchen table. It read:

> The purpose of this note is to thank you for all your friendship, kindness, and hospitality. For picking me up at the airport and letting me stay in your home. And for all the really beautiful conversations about art and life we've had over the years. I know you don't approve of what I'm about to do, and I'm also grateful that you don't approve, that you continue to be a voice of sanity in my life. I ask myself if those have always been our respective roles: you the voice of sanity, me not. So I just want to thank you again and ask you not to worry. Whatever happens, it is what I've come here to do. I think of you as my favourite friend.

However, when I get to the kitchen, there is already a note waiting for me, in an envelope with my name on it. I put the envelope in my pocket and replace it with my handwritten missive. Then I gather my carefully packed belongings and quietly close the front door behind me.

There is a certain joy in being wrong. This is one of the many thoughts I have walking along dark streets toward the outskirts of the city, then past many buildings and houses that back home we would call suburbs, though I don't think they call them that here. In the landscape I would be traversing, along with constant bombings, there were many different groups of various sizes and from various places, all fighting each other, sometimes in coalitions, sometimes alone. There were many checkpoints on the roads, checkpoints for cars and vehicles, but, I had read, if you were travelling alone, by foot, it wasn't especially difficult to avoid them. What I didn't expect was how long I would walk without anything happening. As I walk through the darkness, and keep walking as it bleeds into dawn, in the farthest distance there is a dot, a splotch. I wonder if it's a village or checkpoint, and continue wondering for what seems like many hours, many lifetimes, until finally I reach it, the dot, the splotch, which does, in fact, turn out to be a village—from what I can tell, completely deserted. Most of the houses have been bombed within an inch of their lives. There is almost nothing left. It is still a village, albeit now painfully in ruins. As I walk through, I look down at my feet. There are bloodstains on the ground at irregular intervals. Also burn marks, ash, and rubble. It is remarkable the degree to which the ground appears scorched. I wonder if I should sleep here for the night, but nothing about the idea feels right. I don't know why exactly, but I have a distinct feeling that the people who live here intend to return. As I pass, I consider snooping into a few of the houses, see what's there, if anything, but again feel it would be wrong. They didn't abandon their homes just so I could later explore a museum of bomb-destroyed dwellings. On the way out is a well from which I fill my water bottles, then worry that it might be poisoned, revenge on any scavenger who tries to loot what is left behind. But the water tastes clean. (Of course, I have absolutely no idea what poisoned water tastes like, but I drink it and later feel fine.)

I continue to walk. Soon the village is once again a distant dot, now on the horizon behind me, but as I turn back to glance at it one last time, I might already hear the plane. I stop to be sure, and moments later the first bomb hits. A single plane bombing a deserted, already-destroyed village. The plane comes back around for a second then third load. Why is this plane bombing this emptiness? Does the pilot think there are soldiers hiding there? Does he want to destroy it to such a degree that no one will ever think to return? Before I manage to arrive at anything resembling an explanation, the pilot has already lost interest in the village, is now flying toward me. There's no cover anywhere in sight, so I just stand there, not knowing if the plane will spot me or pass over on its way to a more promising target. My heart is beating faster than I ever remember it doing, and if I'm not killed by a bomb, perhaps a heart attack will finish me off. I wonder if I should run, but there's nowhere to go as the plane speeds past, then circles back around, coming down lower as it circles back for a third time. On the fourth pass I feel it happening, this plane is about to drop a bomb and I look straight up, almost sure it will be the last movement I ever make, when the plane explodes mid-air, whatever is left spiralling downward and crashing maybe fifty feet away. A moment ago I was sure I was dead, and now, here I am, once again alive, in shock.

I consider walking over to examine the wreckage but don't want to push my luck so I continue to stand there, almost paralyzed. I had always thought that if my life was utterly in danger, some primal instinct would kick in and I'd find out whether or not I truly wanted to live. And perhaps it was my survival instinct that froze me where I stood, not making any sudden moves, happy to be passed over, remain unnoticed. But I find the evidence inconclusive and I'm not sure how long I've stared at the flaming, smoking wreckage before I once again begin to walk.

As I walk, something definitive begins to happen within my thoughts (which is rare for me)—a kind of quiet epiphany, a decision, albeit mostly a hypothetical one. Since my friend had accused me of coming here only to write about it—the only one of her accusations I, at the time, felt confident wasn't true, though now I'm no longer so sure—I've started asking myself why and how doing so would be wrong. Was there anything I could do to make it less wrong? Which led to my decision. Because if I do end up writing a book about this—and I'm still not sure I will, still feel it's not the reason I came, not what I'm here for—I decide that in that eventual, imaginary book no one will die. Not a single death. We already know bombs kill people, in wars people die. But I don't want bombs to kill people, I don't want to kill them again by transforming their deaths into prose, don't want to profit from their deaths, don't want someone to say how tragic it all is and that my imaginary book derives resonance from such tragedy. If I write about it, it will be because I'm a writer and, short of dying, I can't seem to help myself. But there's enough death in the world and, as I walk, I decide that I will not add any more.

I remember reading that with the invention of aerial bombing there were many who thought now was the time, this will be the thing that finally puts an end to all wars. How could war possibly flourish when both sides have such bomb-ready overviews of the terrain, could so clearly see and attack the situation? No one would ever have an advantage. Or if one side had bombers and the other did not, then wars would be merciless, brief, and therefore barely worth fighting. This was a perverse kind of technological optimism and also a prediction that has yet to come true. It turns out that though airplanes are useful, battle spaces remain complicated, and there will always be effective combatants without access to the air. Many strategies remain. I'm not here to write a history of war. I am only here to walk. That history is long and my life might be short. There have been many wars; has anyone ever been able to calculate just how many, many slaughters, genocides, conquests, defeats? I have read about only a few, at times feel I have read about a few too many, and I am against all of them. Planes have been dropping bombs and firing missiles for a very long time, though I suppose a somewhat shorter time if one compares it to the entire history of warfare, a history I am not currently writing. War has, of course, changed but seems no closer to ending. It is only more violent and more pointless, much like my trip. A walk across territory over which I will never have any overview. A walk through great violence with little point.

I feel myself losing track of time, try to calculate: I have now walked an entire night and an entire day. I have now walked perhaps more than I have ever walked before in my life, at least in one go, and I'm realizing my exhaustion, realizing I am finally too exhausted to continue. I unroll my sleeping bag under a tree and lie down for the night, trying to sleep for several hours, yet the longer I lie there, the more awake I feel, listening to the distant bombs. I wish I had brought something to read. I can't believe I came on this trip and didn't bring anything to read. It's like I don't know myself at all. Reading is often my main activity and I get anxious when I'm without it. But I suppose I wanted to change myself by coming here, to no longer be the one who reads, no longer be the one who is constantly reading, and instead step away from books and into life. Is it working? Am I in life now? Is this fear I currently feel more like being in life? Would it really have been so bad to bring along a book? And then I realize I do, in fact, have something to read. I have the envelope still in my pocket, the envelope my friend left on the kitchen table. It is now extremely crumpled. I tear it open:

This is my last attempt to describe to you why, from my perspective, what you are planning to do is wrong.

A misguided way of thinking about the world and your role within it. A gesture that does more harm than good. You think you're powerless because you don't see your own power. You have never experienced a collective movement or even a collective moment. You want to learn but you're going about it in the wrong way and therefore cannot help but learn the wrong thing.

When the war started, at first, I spent a great deal of time in a bomb cellar, a deep basement about three blocks from my parents' apartment. I would sit there, on the floor, my knees pressed against my chest, unable to think, unable to read. I would not have described it this way at the time, but, in retrospect, I think I was experiencing an unhealthy amount of self-pity. I would listen to the bombs falling on the buildings that surrounded me. Often I would cry but more often I would be too exhausted to do even that. My parents refused to come to the shelter with me. They said they were dying anyway and it wasn't worth the effort. But I was rarely alone in that cellar. There were never fewer than ten of us crowded into that dark room and often as many as fifty. At the limit we could barely all fit. There were times we would sit in silence, waiting for the coast to be clear so we could walk back up into the light. But there were other times, the times I remember best, when we told each other our stories. It was in that cellar that I lost my isolation. If we were going to possibly die together, then we should, in the meantime, live together as well, as best we could, as closely as possible. But you haven't learned this lesson yet. You still want to walk alone. Alone you can do nothing. You want to learn through the simple act of putting yourself in danger, but what you're going to learn I can already tell you now: that alone you can accomplish nothing. Meaning comes in connection with others.

You want your government to stop dropping bombs on us and actually believe that such a dream is only possible in some fantastical afterlife. But we are stuck here and therefore have no choice but to believe it is possible sooner, in the eventual here and now. Anything else is an abyss of pure despair. Your walking will not bring you closer to us, and it will also not provide the information you are searching for. Be honest with yourself and go back home. Work from there to stop the bombs and don't give up until they've stopped. You know what I'm saying is right. Don't go.

Underneath the words *don't go* she had signed her name. For some reason it was her signature that made me cry. I cry for a while before I finally turn off my flashlight and stare up into the pulsing darkness. For a brief moment I think: this is the story of my life, being told not to do something but doing it anyway, because I think that's what an artist is supposed to do, because on a subconscious level I feel self-sabotage is avant-garde, because I don't know how to help others and therefore will never really know how to help myself. But also, I've always felt self-pity is a garbage emotion. And though everything my friend wrote in her letter is true and full of both anger and deep care for me, and even though I am, of course, reading it too late, already too late, I know I am once again facing a problem with no solution, as I have always done. If I had read her letter before I left, who knows, but I didn't, I'm reading it now, here I am, having put myself in danger, yet with the real danger still to come. Here I am for the first time in my life absolutely unsure what will happen next. I listen again to the bombs falling in the distance as I fold up the letter, put it back in the envelope with my name on it, then put the envelope back in my pocket.

It was several more days of walking, or perhaps more like weeks, before I hit the areas I'd been most warned about. In a car it would have probably taken a day or two, in a plane maybe a few hours. (Also, away from the roads, I was often unsure if I was going in straight lines or in circles. It is most likely I was not taking the shortest route.) On the way, I passed through areas of utter devastation, but also areas of serene beauty. I slid past minor skirmishes, people shooting at each other from the hills, and in the distance so many bombs. Many times I heard gunshots in the distance, and often the distance felt not so far away. I saw bullet holes in walls and trees, so many I lost count, like misplaced punctuation decorating the landscape. At all times I walked toward the distant bombs. I feel I must keep walking as if my life depends on it. I have to keep walking, since the only place to throw good money is after bad.

As I get closer, the scale of the wreckage increases, and I start seeing people more often, mainly children, who stare at me but don't approach. I have brought two maps, one map of the region and a second—a tattered computer print-out—that purported to show where the fighting was heaviest. But as I stare at the maps now it is unclear exactly where I stand. I didn't bring any technology, since there is little or no satellite service here. More importantly, I suppose, I wanted to leave all of that behind. I am staring at the first map, trying to figure out which village I have landed in, when the planes arrive. I look up and there are at least ten as the bombs begin to fall on all sides. I knew this would happen eventually and it is happening now. I look up, hoping at least one of the planes will explode, but none do. This is the closest I've ever been, and the bombs falling so close are like being physically pummelled by air, violence, and sound. I brace myself in the middle of the road so as not to topple toward the ground, which is shaking like an earth-quake from hell, and then I fall, just lie there. The ground shakes as I lie terrified upon it. The low-lying building clos-est to me is hit, the walls collapsing inward, screams coming from inside, flames against the sky, and I can feel the heat on my face like an oven. I lie there paralyzed, wondering if I should stand or keep still. To say I'm afraid doesn't mean anything. I feel a pure animal fear blaring at an intensity so psychotic it is as if my inner life has been shredded in two, as if I'm bleeding tears.

I can't tell how many bombs were dropped or what they destroyed, but the planes dropping them were gone as quickly as they came, hit and run, smoke and dust everywhere in lung-drenching waves. For a long moment I'm not sure if I'm still alive as people run past to clear away rubble. One of the men doing so looks at me, sees me watching him as I slowly stumble back up onto my feet, and gestures me over. I realize I had been staring at them, mesmerized like one might be by a television screen, but his gesture snaps me out of it and I head in, do my best to help. They are working quickly, in careful unison, obviously having done this before, so as I'm lifting away bricks and heaps of drywall I do my best to watch them work, imitate their technique, so much more efficient than mine. We hear screaming, it was there before but we hear it more clearly now, and several men move to find where it's coming from. The screaming again gets louder as they carve a space down toward it. In a few minutes they've uncovered someone, in obvious pain but still alive. He's covered in dirt, caked in thick layers of dust mixed with blood, yet the moment the sunlight hits his face he immediately stops screaming and smiles, a happy-to-be-alive grin. They finish pulling him out, he takes a few moments to stretch his limbs, and soon he's hard at work with the others, still obviously in pain but nonetheless clearing away more rubble. There are several other audible screams and cries for help, buried even deeper, but sooner or later we find them all, alive and shell-shocked—a few children, a wailing infant, two women, all covered head to toe in blood and dust—and when everyone feels confident no one else remains buried, they all stop work as quickly as they began, leaving the rubble where it lies, the one who first gestured toward me shaking my hand before heading off. (In reality, everyone would have been crushed. This book is not reality.) Just as quickly, others are going through the wreckage, teenagers and children, to see what of value they can salvage.

My walking is now filled with the darkest thoughts. Am I simply walking forward through space, across territory, or am I also walking historically forward through time? Simultaneously backward and forward through history? I realize I haven't spoken to anyone since leaving my friend's apartment like a thief in the night, leaving my note and taking with me her more brilliant and eloquent letter (and I'm supposed to be the writer). I start to think about all the stated reasons for this war and other wars like it. For humanitarian reasons (every time an expensive humanitarian bomb landed on civilians, it was enough to turn even the most optimistic Pollyanna into a hardened cynic). To fight communists. To fight terrorists. To stop the spread of communism or terrorism or extremism or something else. To help people. To improve the lot of women. Because we're right and they're wrong. Because: Why do they hate us and why do they hate our way of life? Because war has always existed and will always exist. To increase the quantity of democracy in the world. Because we have a responsibility to the world and to freedom. For freedom. For strategic reasons. To stop a domino from setting off all the other dominoes.

And then I move on to what I think the reasons are for this war and so many others. Because our leaders need therapy. Because a bully needs a victim. Because so-called powerful men are deeply insecure. So politicians in favour of war can get elected or re-elected by voters in favour of war. To make money. To placate the arms industry and their high-priced lobbyists. To justify never-ending increases in the military budget. To distract from rampant domestic problems. To bring certain natural resources and labour into the jurisdiction of the global marketplace. To ensure these resources most benefit the capitalists doing the bombing and least benefit the people being bombed. Because it's easier to kill people who look or sound different than you. Because hatred takes on a life of its own. To explain to the world that you do it our way or suffer the consequences. Because a protection racket needs to constantly ensure no one steps out of line or seeks protection elsewhere. So they can set up permanent military bases to keep the surrounding countries in line. Because there is no alternative. Because there is only room for one empire at a time.

I didn't think it was possible for the destruction to become greater than what I had previously witnessed, but the further I went, the greater the destruction became. Everything gone, half-gone, skeletons of cement and rebar twisted into the ground. Here I do actually see a few anti-aircraft launchers, guarded as if they were made of pure gold, valued and protected for obvious reasons as the only defence against constant attack from the sky. Then, like so many times before, there are bombs. I hear them before I see them, but moments later, I see them clearly as well. I'm at this end of this village while bombs pummel the far edge, easily within walking distance. As I stand, one of the planes explodes mid-air, spontaneously, with no assistance from the anti-aircraft launcher sitting unused for that very purpose. Every time I see one of the planes explode I feel a little surge of joy. But already five or six bombs have made their instant carnage as the remaining planes make their unimpeded escape. I continue to stand paralyzed, endless clouds of dust and debris rolling in my direction. I wonder what I must look like, standing stone-still in the middle of the road, staring straight ahead as if I could stop all this war using only my thoughts. I think long and hard about what I'm actually feeling right now. All I feel is fear. Not even confusion, just fear. Fear and loneliness. I stop looking straight ahead and look around. I realize how little on this trip, so far, I've actually taken in my surroundings. I've been focused on the bombs and yet there is so much more happening all around me. The fear I'm feeling, and must have been feeling since the beginning, is intense. I don't know what to do with such intensity, don't even know how to feel it. All I know how to do is avoid it by trying to think of other things. As I consider this, something else changes, more commotion, gunfire. People in the buildings on one side of the street shooting at the buildings on the other side. I still haven't moved. A man sees me standing in the crossfire and grabs me. The moment he snaps me out of it, I'm running behind him as if for my life, then standing in the front room of some family's home, then crouching behind a pile of furniture meant to protect us from the bullets. A stranger just saved my life and he's now crouching beside me along with many others. As with other firefights over the past week, I don't really know who is shooting at who, which side is which. A bullet hits one of the windows and it shatters. The other windows are already gone. Then soldiers are battering down the door and we're running. I don't exactly understand where there is to run to until I begin to understand. Sections of each wall have been cut away and we're ducking through them, from house to house, gathering others as we go, others who also now realize they need to run, since we have unfortunately drawn the soldiers toward them. But we're no longer running, the territory doesn't allow for it, we're walking as quickly as possible through the cut-open walls from one house to the next, around furniture and the trappings of people's lives, pushing aside a carpet or covering hung down to mask the opening. I've already lost track of how many houses we've moved through. I can feel bullets brush past us from behind, perhaps from ahead as well, and as we rush I feel adrenaline. I didn't come here to feel adrenaline. Or I tell myself I didn't come here to feel adrenaline. But now I feel adrenaline. Great, exhilarating surges of the stuff. It's only moments until we've run out of houses, turn, head out a back door, and almost as quickly our group scatters in all directions. I look over and realize the man who first saved me, pulling me from the crossfire, is still standing beside me and I want to thank him, but as I reach to shake his hand he's hit, or has already been hit, on his shirt I see blood. As I reach over to shake his hand he falls forward and I clumsily catch him, almost toppling backward under his weight but managing to brace myself. There's more blood than I first thought. My hands, arms, and chest are completely covered. He's not dead. After I've held him for a moment, he steps away. His family—I assume they're his family—have come back around, pulling him from my arms. I watch them turn the corner, almost certain I'll never see them again as I fall back against the wall behind me, shell-shocked and exhausted, starting to wipe my face but then realizing my hand is covered in blood. I instead wipe the blood on my pant leg. I came here because I felt I had blood on my hands, but now I literally have blood on my hands. I wonder if I've been shot as well but am not sure I can tell. I listen; gunfire is coming from every direction. As I keep listening it starts to move farther away. I can't tell how long all of that took. I didn't even speak to the man who saved my life and it feels so unbearably stupid that he was hit while I wasn't. If, in fact, I wasn't. That I'm covered in his blood instead of my own.

After another day or so of walking, there is a river and I wash off the dried blood as best I can. It has been such a hot summer here. The smell of dried blood has been making me nauseous and it feels good to be at least partly free of it. I'm filthy from head to toe and the river only partly does the job. I rinse out my clothes and lay them in the sun. My pants are still ripped from climbing over the fence to get to the secret art party, a party that already seems like many lifetimes ago. When I walk, there are long stretches with few or no people, and where there are no people, there is also no fighting. Or, at least, that's what I tell myself. But I can always hear it. Or not always, though I barely notice when it starts or stops, since it is also now a constant dull roar in my ears.

I sit and watch the river. The water rushes calmly along as if everything is all right in the world. I find it almost unbearable that so close to all the surrounding fighting and commotion there could be such a peaceful spot, sitting under the shade of a tree watching the patient flow of the river. I don't know why I say unbearable, it was simply the first word that came to mind. Staring at the water, I start to calm down a little, which makes me more aware of how much

stress I've been holding in my body. I've never been especially interested in nature. But there is this river in front
of me, and it is the first thing I've looked at for any length
of time in many days where I don't also feel they might
immediately bomb it. Who would possibly bomb a small
river? I start to think about the blood I just washed out of
my clothes, about the man who rushed out into the street to
pull me from the crossfire. He really didn't need to do that.
He probably saved my life, definitely at the risk of his own,
and asked nothing in return. I wonder what he was thinking.
(He was probably thinking how stupid I was to be standing
there in the line of fire. Or maybe that I was paralyzed by
shock and clearly needed assistance.) He knows nothing
about me and I know nothing about him. Then again, he's
living in war, must risk his life all the time, purposefully
or otherwise. You see a person in danger and simply rush
forward to save their life. You don't think. It's not a philosophical moment. You have a split second to act and you act.
And in that way it is also a philosophical moment. I think
again, and over again, about that split-second moment in
which he saved me, and his action seems almost the opposite of how I've lived my entire life. Over and over again I
stopped to think, to drift, to daydream, to consider, while
moment after moment passed me by. I suppose one might
say I was daydreaming when he saved my life. Or not exactly
daydreaming but paralyzed, which often seems to me to be
more or less the same thing. And walking is another form of
daydreaming. When I think this way, despite having come
here, I can't help but feel that I still don't know what I'm
talking about. I hope he's still alive. (But of course he's still
alive, because in this book no one dies.)

Staring at the river, I start to pay more attention to how
I'm feeling. I don't feel well at all, like I've been poisoned

followed by a physical beating. My breathing is laboured, most likely from all the dust and debris, but perhaps also from a sense of pure, sustained panic. I have travelled, come here. I am not having a transformative experience. The water flows past me and I watch, processing so many things at once I can barely think straight. This is a quiet, contemplative moment—perhaps my last for a while, or ever—and I should use it to put my thoughts in order, but instead I sleep for a few hours, don't recall having any particular dreams, but if I did, wonder if they were dreams about walking or war. Or dreams that had absolutely nothing to do with walking or war, since in your dreams at least you can momentarily escape your current situation. Or transform it into something unrecognizable, something more peaceful or more frightening, something that unnerves with questions it raises but cannot answer. This book is not reality but neither is it a dream. I'm not even sure how long I slept. Now that I'm awake I can think of nothing else to do but repack my things, continue walking. I notice my clothes are still ever-so-slightly damp as I put them back on, hoping the sun will dry them on my way.

Up ahead, in what is rapidly becoming an almost daily ritual, I see a village. I try to count in my head how many villages I've now been through. A few were so small I'm not sure you could even call them villages, I don't know what to call them. And a few were large enough to be cities. Most had seen fighting, but it also seemed possible a few had not. (Why do I always want to write "not yet"?) And between each one, I was walking more than I have ever walked in my life. Each time I get closer I can tell right away whether there has been serious bombing, and this time I see there has not. I stop and look at the buildings ahead of me, finding them more beautiful out of fear they might soon be destroyed, as moments later everything goes black. I think I've passed out but hear commotion around me. I'm being roughly grabbed and lifted up. I can feel myself being carried away, and cry out. In response several voices shout at me. I hear the words *kidnap* and *ransom* and immediately go limp. The men carrying me, it feels like there are two of them, are clearly strong enough. They carry me smoothly and with little effort, though carrying a live body can never be completely without awkwardness. As two of them carry me, a third, with great effort, gaffer-tapes my hands behind my back. He really manages to bind them tight. A voice tells me to be quiet, stop squirming, and I don't know why but I instantly comply. Again he says the word *ransom*. Previously I had thought I wanted to die but now I definitely know that I don't want to be kidnapped. As I'm being carried, I'm also trying to understand what's happening. There is a bag over my head. There are several small air holes in the bag and I'm having only minimal difficulty breathing. As I was standing there these men must have recognized me as a foreigner and thought they could get good money for me. Or maybe they had been following me for a while, waiting for the right moment to enact their plan. I wonder if they'll have any luck or if I'll survive the process. I can't see anything but I hear intense commotion. Then it feels like I'm being shoved into something, I hear a trunk slam down on top of me. A long pause in which nothing happens, then the engine starts up as we pull away. In the trunk it's considerably more difficult to breathe. The remaining dampness in my clothes constricts me and irritates my skin, giving me chills. I worry I'm going to vomit, knowing this would be absolutely the worst situation in which to do so. Everything is pitch black, a claustrophobic darkness I don't remember having experienced in my life, the heat unbearable, and I'm curled into a ball, thinking this is probably what I deserve for deciding to make such a stupid journey in such a stupid way. Waves of panic followed by a kind of giving up, there's nothing to do and panicking certainly won't help, followed by more waves of panic. We drive for what seems an infinitely long time and now I really do pass out, or at least pass in and out of consciousness. When I come to, one of the times I come to, still half-conscious, my first thought is that now everything is clear: my luck has finally run out. My life will end in the trunk of this car or shortly after the trunk is opened. I can clearly hear the conversation up front as we drive, but it's in languages I don't understand. It sounds like debate, arguing over where they should take me or maybe arguing about matters even more banal. I then realize, or at least think I realize, when they grabbed me they managed to get my bag and they were going though it item by item. I try to remember what I have in there. Several mostly empty water bottles. A flashlight. My two maps. Food and a little bit of money. A small notebook in which I have written almost nothing. What I don't have is a phone or credit card, two things they might be looking for, things they might be able to sell. The only ID I have is still in my pocket along with a folded newspaper article and my friend's crumpled letter. In their voices I think I hear irritation and wonder if it's irritation that there's nothing of value in my bag and nothing to identify me. I, of course, have absolutely no idea who they are or why they thought to kidnap me, but for the first time it strikes me that they possibly have no idea who I am either and therefore no idea how little I'm worth. I believe I pass out again, or at least sleep for a while, and when I come to I soon find myself considering what kind of measurement could possibly gauge how long we've been driving, maybe a day or longer, or maybe only a few hours. The car begins to slow and I hear my captors swearing. At least I assume they're swearing, they're clearly unhappy about something. It's only when the car begins to slow that I realize we've been driving in almost complete silence at least since I last awoke. We move a few feet forward, then stop, move a few feet forward, then stop. It continues. I try to guess what's going on and it occurs to me we're now in a queue, most likely the lineup for a checkpoint. There have been many checkpoints I've so far managed to avoid, travelling by foot. I wonder if when we get to the actual checkpoint I should start screaming, if it will do me any good. I have a great deal of time to mull over this question as the car moves forward a few feet more then stops, moves forward a few feet more then stops, moves forward a few feet more then stops. Should I start screaming or not start screaming—which one is more likely to get me killed? When we finally do get to what I assume is the checkpoint, it happens so quickly I don't have time to decide. There are voices speaking loudly, directly over the trunk, moments before the trunk is opened and I'm roughly pulled out, my body so cramped I can barely stand. Suddenly everything is very still. The people holding me up, one on each side, aren't moving at all. I can feel the fear in their bodies as they hold me, their fingernails cutting into my arms, doing their best to keep me upright and still. An endlessly long moment of silence during which I can't hear or see a thing but I'm imagining a standoff, everyone pointing guns at everyone else, frozen with their fingers on the triggers, one sudden movement and bullets will start flying, a hostage with a bag over his head in the middle of it all. (If there's anything worse than an unreliable narrator, it's an unreliable narrator with a bag over his head.) I then hear a voice through a bullhorn saying, "Surrender and you will not be harmed." Then saying what I believe is the exact same thing in another language. Then saying the same thing again in yet another language. I realize it is only a recording and hope the soldiers holding the bullhorn, playing the recording, are going to save me but somehow know they are not. There is another long moment of stillness until I barely know or understand what is happening. My captors, or someone, pull the bag off my head. The light is blinding, disorienting, as they show my face to the enemy, in the process making what is, in my opinion, a very reasonable guerrilla-military decision, to use me as a human shield, thinking my fellow countrymen will be reluctant to shoot one of their own. It becomes immediately apparent my fellow countrymen feel no such reluctance. If the correct response is "Don't make any sudden moves," the sudden move of pulling the bag from my head sets everything in motion. I have been walking, am unwashed, covered in dirt, dust, and filth, am probably unrecognizable to the soldiers who immediately start firing at me. If they had recognized me I'm not sure it would have made any difference. As I fall roughly to the ground, I hear gunfire from all directions, then moments later bombs or missiles or some other kind of explosions, most likely aimed at those who, for such a short time, had been my kidnappers and yet treated me reasonably well in their custody. If they had held on to me for longer, it's possible the treatment would have worsened. But in that short time I never felt they wanted to harm me—they only wanted ransom. Maybe the explosions I hear have nothing to do with us. I listen to them more closely and they sound too far away, just another chapter in the never-ending bombardment I have walked through without reason. Lying here on the ground, in the dirt, pretending to be dead, or already dead, I'm not sure which, I am filled with an overwhelmingly absurd emotion: sadness that they never got their ransom, that I'll never know what amount they managed to get for me. When everyone started shooting they dropped me and ran, firing back over me, pushed me toward my firing countrymen and ran. The people who kidnapped me ran and those who may or may not have shot me ran after them. Maybe not shooting at me, only past me, at the others who were fleeing and I got in the way. Or simply shooting everything in their path. If I was really dead I wouldn't know I was dead, but I don't know so I must be. I feel each bullet lodged in my body, feel that they are fatal. My journey has barely begun. Is it really a good idea for me to die this soon? But that doesn't matter because I'm dead. Because this book isn't reality and neither is it finished. This book is not reality. Reality is much, much worse.

2: Care and Time

I raise my hands slowly, as if I'm in a bad Hollywood movie surrounded by bullshit hero cops. Did they know what this gesture meant? Was it a universal gesture? Had they even seen bad Hollywood movies here? Of course they had, they've seen them fucking everywhere. I was being stupid and condescending, but in my defence such thoughts were inspired by pure and visceral fear. As I lifted my arms above my head I could feel my rib cage ache, feel again how much pain I was in, how the trip so far had mainly been like receiving a physical beating. And then it struck me: the seven women and three men currently pointing guns at me were the actual reason I was here. Not the actual reason, more like my fantasy of the actual reason. I didn't think I'd find them and, even if I did find them, saw no reason they would trust me or let me stay with them. So far my anxieties were proving correct. They did not trust me. I had stumbled into their ambush, their routine patrol, had my hands in the air, they were pointing their rifles at me, and that was as far as we'd gotten.

One of the men comes around behind me and pats me down, then goes through my bag with great care. When he is done, everyone lowers their weapons and I ask if I can take something from my pocket, pointing to my pocket as I do so, then withdrawing the now extremely tattered article. I carefully unfold it, hold it up, and can tell right away that they recognize themselves in the picture. I thought I would get lost, and I did get lost, but at the same time I followed

49

my maps and walked more or less directly here. I knew I had a destination, but at the same time I didn't believe I had a destination, or didn't want to have a destination, but here I was at the place I was actually most curious about in the entire world, a place that I absolutely believed might have concrete things to teach me.

It is completely understandable that they do not want their names, their location, their military techniques, or the names of any of their organizations, or any of the many branches and sub-branches of these organizations, published in this book. This book is not reality. I am attempting to write about all of this in a way that keeps secrets, that attempts to ensure no harm will come to them. (Observations not directly related to defence I am free to report on as generously and openly as my abilities allow.) They trusted me, I still do not know why, and my dream is to never betray this trust.

In fact, this story shouldn't even be about me. It should be entirely about them. To put it all a little bit too simply: they are endlessly inspiring and courageous while I am obviously not. But I'm a writer and therefore can only write what I know and imagine. I stayed with them for about a year. I now clearly remember that the first thing they did was take me to a hospital. I was generally reluctant to go to the hospital back home, because, of course, I could barely afford it. Here many spoke at least a little bit of the same language as me or I was able to communicate through translators. I'm certainly not able to communicate with everyone. At the hospital the doctors confirmed that I had been shot twelve times by that firing squad of my fellow countrymen but miraculously none of the wounds were fatal (because this book isn't reality), though many had become seriously infected. The doctors worked efficiently, they had for obvious reasons treated millions of bullet wounds since the start of the war, and I was assured that the wounds were now properly cleaned and bandaged.

"This is liberated territory," Goldman explains to me, "but, really...I ask myself every single day: who knows for how long." (For reasons I believe are self-explanatory, I have replaced names of the most discussed revolutionaries and citizens I met over the course of that year with names of historical revolutionaries, organizers, and anarchists.) "There's what everyone seems to want to call civil war to the south of us, both sides repeatedly bombed by your country and their coalition of the willing. Being bombed rather indiscriminately, if you don't mind me saying so." I replied that of course I agreed. "In fact, the more I think about it, the more time goes by, the more I realize it's the most cowardly and pathetic form of intervention. More cowardly bombing: killing many, risking nothing. All it does is prolong the war and prove your government doesn't care how many civilians they kill, as long as neither side ever wins and things continue on like this indefinitely. It's a kind of divide and conquer, the oldest tricks are the meanest, as long as they're fighting each other they won't find a road toward meaningful self-rule and the region remains unstable and, therefore, through some sick political logic, less threatening." I continue to agree as Goldman continues to explain. "And then to the north, who knows what's going to happen. Right now it's mainly an embargo, nothing comes in and nothing goes out, but I'm sure they'd be more than happy to begin bombing us as well. For the moment they're holding their fire, perhaps in the hopes that our wonderful experiment will fail under the weight of its own contradictions. Or that others will do the bombing for them and save them the ammunition. But for now, at least, we're still liberated territory and we have to make the most of it while we have the chance. Do you understand?" I say that I do.

Goldman was the one who spent the most time with me, their official spokesperson as far as I was concerned. I believe she was assigned to me because of her language skills—of the many commanders she was perhaps the one who had been speaking my language the longest, for reasons she never explained she had learned it as a child, and it was only a few times over the course of the entire year I said a word she didn't know. So often she would speak to me with her Kalashnikov slung over her shoulder, like it was a part of her and she didn't feel quite right without it.

I'd already told her I didn't know how to fire a gun, and she laughed at me, carefully explaining that if I was going to go out on patrol with them I had to be able to hold my own. So they gave me a rifle, noticeably in disrepair, and after a week of training told me I was on my own but that I really had to practise. My life might be on the line if I didn't. Every morning it was the same thing. I fire at the target (the side of an old barn with black-and-white circles within circles painted on it) and I miss. I fire again at the target. Again I miss. Every morning I would come here and fire at the target but only very occasionally would I hit it. When I did it mostly felt like an accident. It was a daily comedy of inaccurate aim. Nonetheless, I thought I was getting better at holding and pointing the gun, of making it look like I knew what I was doing. I wondered if such appearances would help on patrol.

One morning Goldman watched me practise and laughed every time I missed. She laughed a lot that morning. In her laughter I heard something I knew was true: if I had been born here, if our roles were reversed and I had lived her life instead of mine, I probably wouldn't have survived. But if I had been born here, perhaps I would have also been taught how to use a gun at a younger age, when I was more malleable and able to learn. Then I realize it wouldn't have made a difference. I was taught a variety of sports as a child yet was terrible at all of them. Back then I could rarely get the ball into the basket and now I can only very rarely get the bullet into the centre of the target. I feel a sense of accomplishment if I even manage to nick the edges. Every morning after target practice I feel incredibly depressed, but it's a different kind of depression than my usual flavour. It has a point, a clear focus: that I'm unable to improve at this very specific task.

That morning Goldman spent warmly laughing at me. After I worked (and missed) my way through my daily allotment of practice bullets, we went for a walk together down by the river. It startled me almost into epiphany when I realized this was the same river, the same river I had washed my clothes in and slept beside, only that part of the river was miles away in the middle of a war zone and this part was right here in the middle of liberated territory. Goldman was remarkably hopeful despite the almost insurmountable difficulties they faced. I have never been particularly optimistic or hopeful in spite of my relatively easy life. "That article says we're a 'thin strip of land,' but almost two million people live here." My attention was strangely split between what Goldman was saying and the river beside me. We walked alongside it. "I joined when I was fifteen. And, I don't always know why, I certainly didn't always know why at the time, but it was quite easy for me to rise, to become a commander. The women who fight with us, with me, we've found ways to build trust, to work together, we're literally fighting for our lives, for our freedom. On either side of us there are dictators and when we fight we're fighting for this little oasis of real freedom in the middle of this landscape of fear and torture and unfreedom. When on all sides the governments work by killing and intimidating their citizens, the idea of not having a government suddenly doesn't seem so far-fetched. I don't think I could fight to invade, to conquer anyone, like so many others do, but we fight in self-defence and that I think I will always be able to do. Over the last twelve years, actually only more recently, I've begun to ask myself other kinds of questions. If it's different for me to kill, to be a soldier, than it is for a man to do the exact same thing. I feel I'm part of a more recent, or even a more important, history. When we kill, to defend ourselves, I often think it means something different than when men do the same."

I started calculating her age—fifteen years plus another twelve—and realized how much younger than me she is. She looks younger, but when she spoke she sounded more like an adult. The river continued to run past us as we walked. I was finding it difficult to process everything I was seeing and experiencing here, everything I was told, to sort out what I believed from what I was skeptical about. I had, of course, never killed anyone, in self-defence or for any other reason. She continued: "We wish we had the power to make planes explode mid-air but we actually have no idea. We're as ignorant about how it's happening as you are. For everyone else it seems it's a problem, an ongoing concern, but for us, since we have no planes, it's really not anything we spend time worrying about. We have more immediate worries."

It was around this time Zana asked if I had brought a tape recorder with me. I hadn't. To Zana this made no sense. I'd come here to write a book. (I don't think I ever said I'd come to write a book, but through hearsay and rumour, everyone eventually assumed this to be the case. I did not come here to write a book. I came for almost opposite reasons.) According to Zana, if I was writing a book, I surely wanted to interview people, and if I was interviewing people, I surely wanted as accurate a record of the conversations as possible. It is perhaps only now I realize how important that moment was. How I wasn't planning to write anything. I didn't come here to write. But then Zana handed me the tape recorder. And it seemed to me in the moment that even if I never wrote about any of it, having the tape recorder was nonetheless a good pretext to talk to as many of those who lived here as possible, and speaking with them was the only way I would learn anything. If I wasn't here to learn, for what other reason could I possible be here? The very first interview was with Zana. And maybe, because it was the first, it has a special place in my heart (though I've never thought of myself as much of an interviewer):

—I don't usually use a recorder.

—Well...you usually write fiction.

—And if I write about my time here. You don't think it should be fiction?

—What we're experiencing here, what I hope you have a chance to experience as well—even though it will be different for you because you didn't help create it and you're probably not planning to stay—but I think you can already see that it's really beautiful and important. So even if you're planning to turn it into fiction, I think there should be a record of it more directly, of our voices.

—Tell me about how you see it.

—Everyone has a say. We need to find, to build, to discover our common values together. As we go.

—And what are those values? From your perspective?

—Well...there are the obvious ones: feminism, ecology, what we might call democracy, for lack of a better word. A different kind of democracy than the one you have where you live. But from my perspective, that's not the most interesting part. Or it is the most interesting part, but because of where it leads.

—Where does it lead?

—I'm talking about how to live, how we live. It leads to a sense that you can live in a way that feels... I'm realizing I still don't know exactly the right word.

—If you don't know the right word then I certainly don't know the right word.

—We're still finding the right words. We're still in that process.

—Any words you use will be good enough for me.

—I'm not sure what the word is for this, but it's the sense that if we keep living this way there will be a hopeful future. And if we don't there won't be. I have never felt anything like that before. We could also say it's a kind of lived free-dom. A sense of movement toward a place where people know how to work together, how to treat each other, where we're replenishing the land instead of destroying it. I mean... people here are still human. There's still jealousy and mistrust and every shade of human shortcoming. But there's also another thing, more unfamiliar.

—Can you explain to me the system of councils? I have to admit, so far I find it all rather complex and confusing.

—It's just a way for things to start at the bottom and filter upward. For everyone to be part of how decisions are made. You have a small, manageable neighbourhood council, and then a larger community council that might represent several neighbourhoods, and then a larger city council where all the community councils come together, bringing with them questions and proposals, many of which began at the neighbourhood level. And the departments are, we might say, also a kind of council. I'm part of the agriculture department, and we work together on a larger plan for agriculture across the entire region—which, as you already know, is based on permaculture, that's the basis for our approach—and we work independently on our field of expertise, but we're also accountable to all of the smaller councils, our staff comes from the councils but we also need to do the rounds and present our plans to each of them, to explain ourselves. And if anyone feels we have it all wrong, we really need to be accountable. There needs to be discussion and we need to keep discussing until everyone understands why we have taken the approach that we have. Even if everyone doesn't agree, they at least have to understand, or there at least has to be that attempt on our part. I'm working on these questions, on how to have enough food for everyone in a way that actually replenishes the soil and lets the livestock be healthy and thrive, that leaves it all better for future generations than we originally found it. I've been working on this since the beginning. But when the situation arises, I can also easily give projects over to someone else who is more qualified or who has better ideas. For me that's not a problem. What's important is the larger project. And that we're all working together on it. That it's open enough for everyone to eventually understand and, if they want, to become involved.

—I assume this would all be easier if you weren't constantly under attack.

—No one ever changed the world by doing what was easy.

—Are there times you fear for your life?

—Of course. If you listen right now you can even hear the bombings. That's always in the background. But that's not what's important. In the grand scheme of things my life isn't so important.

—What's important then?

—That our project survives long enough to serve as a positive example for the rest of the world.

Zana took me to many farms, many different kinds of farms. Not all of them were based on permaculture, but in her vision of the future, her hope for the future, sooner or later most of them would be. I know nothing about farming, permaculture or otherwise. So I often didn't understand what I was looking at, even as it was being carefully explained to me. Every once in a while I had to remind myself that they had done all of this in less than ten years. So often the farm animals roamed free, gobbling up any harmful pests, removing the need for pesticides, and their animal freedoms seemed analogous to some of the other freedoms that were being embodied and experienced all around me.

I know I need to change. That I need to be changed by the experiences of being here. Why would I even come here if I wasn't open enough to being changed by the generosity of the experience? (The journey to get here was certainly not easy. And who knows if I survived.) On a page in my small notebook I write the words *practical utopia*. This is the most concise way I've found of understanding it. This is what I want to believe I'm experiencing here, and there is so much evidence to support my desire. At the same time I know I'm being handled, I'm being managed. That I mainly see what I'm shown, that I mainly hear what is translated for my benefit. Still there is a feeling, a spirit in the air. It's undeniable. Everywhere you go, you can so clearly feel and sense it. I can't possibly imagine how it could be false, which certainly doesn't mean I have all the necessary information.

Why I choose to turn the tape recorder on sometimes yet not others remains an ongoing mystery for me. Was it a feeling, a feeling that I was about to hear something good? Or did the impulse come from them, they saw I had the recorder, perhaps unconsciously glanced down at it, and that was my (equally unconscious?) cue to start recording. There were so many conversations I wish I had recorded that I didn't and so many other conversations I wish I hadn't recorded that I did. I had a finite number of tapes and did my best to make every tape count, but my methods of doing so were erratic and lacking in finesse. Most of the recorded conversations were in favour of everything that was happening here, those were the individuals who were most often brought to me, or who I was introduced to, but there was the occasional not-in-favour individual who slipped through the cracks:

—I'm not sure I understand what you're saying.

—I feel it's my home and I should be able to sell it if I so choose.

—You're not allowed to sell your house?

—That's the law now. I'm not allowed.

—But you do own it?

—Yes, I own it. But the way the law works now, I only own it for as long as I live there. When I don't live there anymore, I no longer own it.

—Interesting. I didn't know that.

—I understand the logic behind it. It's to prevent speculation. It's all been explained to me clearly and earnestly. But I live there. I lived there before this territory was "liberated"—as they now like to say—and therefore I believe I should maintain the same rights I had before. That I've always had.

—Why do you want to sell your house?

—I don't.

—What do you mean?

—I don't want to sell my house. It's the principle of the matter. I just feel it should be allowed.

—Would you describe yourself as a capitalist?

—No, that's not the way I see it. That's not the point. I understand that we're now living in this experiment and I can more or less go along. I certainly prefer living here to anywhere else in the region. But it's an experiment. That means the rules are still in progress. Which means they're still up for debate. That's all I'm doing: calling some of these rules into question.

—Why would you prefer to live here than anywhere else?

—How do you mean?

—You said you'd prefer to live here than anywhere else in the region.

—I've lived here my entire life. I've always lived here. My parents lived here. Their parents lived here.

—Is that the only reason?

—I'm not sure I understand what you're asking.

—I'm just wondering if the experiment, the fact that this territory is now liberated, is in any way part of the reason you prefer living here.

—Look, I'm not against the experiment...

—But you're not particularly in favour of it either.

—I'm considering it. I'm not immune to learning from my surroundings. And it seems to me that it might still go in many different directions. But even that's not the point. Because I'm part of it. I live here too. I can make my case and find out how many others agree.

—Are there other things you want to push for? Other than selling your house.

—I need to be careful how I go about it. You need to pick your battles. I think there's a lot of people like me who believe they should still have the right to sell their house if they choose, so I decided that was the best place to start.

—But if you end up making progress on that issue, you might later move on to other questions.

—I don't know. We'll have to see how it goes.

I attended many meetings. Everything here takes place in the form of a meeting. There was the meeting to discuss how to distribute the excess supply of wheat created by particularly good crops that year and the meeting to discuss a program in which women who didn't feel safe at night could be walked home by other women who were armed. And then another meeting to discuss a program to simply arm all women in order to make the previously mentioned program unnecessary. (A memorable quote I jotted down from that meeting: "If we're going to train women to shoot, we should also train them to aim for the genitals. That would really be an effective deterrent." My translator was laughing when she translated this, laughing so hard I could barely understand what she was saying. Many in the room were laughing and it was difficult to ascertain how serious a proposition it was. My feeling was that it was serious in its intent but not necessarily in execution. I wanted to laugh along with them, but for some reason I couldn't. I of course knew exactly what the reason was. But I did want to laugh. I can so clearly remember the feeling.)

I press down on the Record button (we were working through a translator so I've edited out certain misunderstandings due to translation):

—What's hard for people to understand is that we liberated this territory peacefully.

—Why do you think that's hard for people to understand?

—I suppose revolution and violence must be connected in people's imaginations. Even when you just hear the word, you think of something like the French Revolution, of the guillotine. But we were fortunate, we got lucky, so that's not the way it happened here. Of course, I have nothing against the reasonable use of violence when it's put toward a good cause. Or in self-defence, which is now so much a part of our daily life, with the patrols and everything. But I think it's important to know that there can still be other ways.

—I have to admit, I still don't completely get it. How it was even possible. It seems almost too good to be true.

—What you have to understand is that we had been organizing for years, in preparation. On the level of each street, neighbourhood to neighbourhood. There had been weekly meetings. We learned about self-organizing.

About meeting in small and then larger groups, learning how to make decisions together. So when the government collapsed, collapsed due to the pressures of war on all sides, we were ready. We could self-organize, ensure all of us had enough food, that the garbage was collected, that we all had heat in the winter. Conditions were therefore almost immediately better here than in any of the battlegrounds that surrounded us. And so, when there were soldiers from the surrounding wars who wanted to stop all this from happening, to stop us from making our own way, we already had the language to speak to them. They could put down their weapons, stay with us, live this experiment alongside us, which many chose to do. Because it was relatively safe and stable here, especially in comparison with everything else, anyone with eyes could see it. Or they could leave peacefully, we wouldn't harm or stop them, the one stipulation being that they had to leave their weapons behind. Many of the weapons we still use to defend ourselves came from those leaving soldiers. They even left behind heavy artillery. So we liberated this territory through self-organization and dialogue.

—Would this have been possible if the government didn't collapse?

—No, maybe not. It's hard to say. If things had been different, then things would have been different. The point is there was an opportunity, a historical moment. We were prepared for it, had been preparing for years, and we rose to the challenge.

—But you did already have weapons. Did every single encounter resolve peacefully? Some of those forces must have still wanted to fight.

—It's really amazing how few casualties there were. I still feel a little spark of pride when I think of it. Less than a hundred. And you have to remember almost two million people live here. But yes, a few wanted to fight. When they were killed, their subordinates could very quickly be brought to see reason. I'm not against violence. I am against cycles of violence, cycles of revenge. Many of us were tortured under the old regime, almost all of us have had loved ones killed in battle. There are many martyrs. I mean, I can only speak for myself, but I also believe I speak for many of us when I say I no longer want revenge. We're now building a different kind of society where it's possible to live well, to live one's self-actualization and to feel what it's like to live freedom, to live in control of one's communal fate. This is a prize so much better than any petty revenge.

—Do you think the peaceful nature of liberating this territory was essential to how things are running now? Would this all still be possible if the takeover, by necessity, had been more violent?

—You really seem to like asking questions like that.

—Like what?

—If this would have been different, what would have happened? If that had been different, what would have happened? I mean, who knows. Everything that happens creates an opening, but an opening isn't enough. You need to see the opening, see what it is, have the solidarity and preparation and communal insight to walk through it and then face what's on the other side. If things had been different, things would have been different. The first step is that we decided we were no longer interested in fighting to build yet another nation-state. We wanted something else. We self-organize on the level of the neighbourhood, from neighbourhood to neighbourhood, and then all the neighbourhoods need to find a way, create structures, for all of us to work together. So when soldiers march in, the entire neighbourhood is already against them. And then the next one and the next one as well. How to organize not toward but against top-down power. Because the state always ends up siding with the capitalists and the capitalists then end up siding with the dictators, because they think they'll make more money that way. So to answer your question, I don't know how to answer your question. We had the courage to take the first step, and then it was almost a matter of luck, but violence wasn't actually necessary. Very little.

—You've used the word *luck* a few times now. Do you really believe in luck?

—I mean, you make your own luck. But you still need some things to go your way. So many things are out of your control and you need some of those things to go your way. Some of the things that are out of your control need to go your way.

—Why do you think the government collapsed?

—I'm not even sure they collapsed. They got scared. They lost their nerve. Specific individuals got scared, lost their nerve, packed up, and ran away.

—Does that have anything to do with luck? Does luck have something to do with not losing your nerve?

—I've never thought of it that way before. You might be

right. Luck might definitely have something to do with not losing your nerve. You have to be able to look the moment in the eyes, know you're not alone, and think: we're really going to do this.

—Luck requires nerve.

—You make your own luck. You can't make it alone, you have to make it all together. But there's always the possibility that the bullet with your name on it will miss you by less than an inch. That's when you know you really can't back down.

There was one particular meeting I will always remember. It was a large meeting, though it was never explained to me why so many people came. A crowded room on a hot summer day. Everyone sweating. There was a translator sitting beside me, but people were often speaking overtop of each other, so she could not translate everything, and at times I was unsure if she was translating the person currently speaking or still working on the person who had last spoken, the overlapping voices all translated into the same voice, transitions between speakers lost in the process. I now feel I'm being unfair. The meeting, especially near the beginning, was a kind of organized chaos and it was clear she was doing her best. I was listening hard. Someone was speaking about coffee, then someone else was speaking about oil for a generator. At the same time, or so it seemed to me, one person was talking about flour, about baking flour, while another was asking about planks of wood. I was trying to understand what all these things had in common: coffee, heating oil, flour, and wood. It turned out it was obvious but it wasn't yet coming to me. My mind wandered, I started to wonder how many people were packed into this room, counting a section of it and then multiplying that section by another estimated number. I decided there were about three hundred of us, as some of these three hundred asked questions about bricks, bread, cellphones, soap, bicycles, vegetables, sheep, radios, wool, and automobile parts.

And then a woman really took the floor. It was amazing the way suddenly everyone was listening to her. For the first time in my life I saw how being able to speak to a room, to hold the attention of a large group of people, was a natural talent. Or maybe not a natural talent, perhaps a talent she had gradually learned over time, through practice and experience. It did seem to me she had an implicit ability to do this, to make the room surround her. The translator was just catching up. She was saying, "We need to be certain that no cartels and monopolies are beginning to form, that everything remains transparent. There are laws about what things should cost, in relation to supply and in relation to prices before liberation. But these aren't laws that can be enforced, they are guidelines that everyone must, in general, agree to follow for the good of the communal project. The purpose of these guidelines is so everyone can afford the things they most need, can have a good life within their means. We are under blockade. The things we most have are things we can produce ourselves and, as we all already know, we must work to produce and process all that we can." (For the purposes of this book, I will call this woman Huerta, replacing her real name with the name of a historical revolutionary, organizer, or anarchist to protect her identity. So those who might want to see the natural leaders of this liberated territory killed will not know which ones to kill. Or, at least, will not know simply by reading this book.)

Huerta said that first she wanted to speak "to those who

have things to sell. If her own department has to constantly be checking that everything they sold was sold at a fair price they couldn't do so. They didn't have nearly enough staff for such a task. Therefore it could never be a question of enforcement, but a question of understanding and good-will. They might think when they are selling something that to raise the price one or two per cent can do no harm, what harm can one or two per cent do, it is such a small amount. But they must ask themselves harder questions, try to look at the larger situation. If they raise their prices one or two per cent, everyone else will feel they have to do the same, and then that process will repeat, and repeat again. We suspect that certain businesses might be col-luding with each other but we don't yet have proof. If you bring us proof of price fixing we will react. We cannot let businesses work together to undermine the public good. But that is not where the real solution lies. The real solution lies in everyone understanding why life here, as difficult as it may be, must continue to remain affordable."

I thought back to the man who wanted the right to sell his house. Clearly a certain line had been drawn and he was trying to move it. I asked myself: What is this line actu-ally about? Is it a line about having things for your own personal use, so you can live, so you can have a good life, versus owning them to further accumulate wealth? Owning them to use versus owning them to profit? I thought of an Indigenous saying I once heard: there is enough for every-one but not enough for everyone's greed. He just wanted the right to sell his house. It was so slippery the way he claimed he didn't actually want to sell his house, which he had inherited from his parents, he only wanted the right to perhaps one day do so. Testing the waters. Checking if it was possible to inch your toe just a little bit over the line before considering the next move. Just two or three per cent. But what is the principle that needs to be defended? That life is meant to be lived and shared, not stockpiled in some bank account. That if you have enough you should enjoy it instead of constantly wanting more.

Huerta is going on to explain that "it is also important to speak to those who want to buy things, which is basically everyone." This gets a big laugh. (I don't know why the fact that everyone wants to buy things is funny but I find myself laughing too.) The translator finds it much easier now that only one person is speaking, her translation measured and clear, full of nuance. "There are guidelines for the price of things, and each of us must work to more fully understand the calculations that inform these guidelines. Every time you make a purchase, you should think about the price. If you think it's too high, you can come speak with us, speak to our department. But there is another point I want to make, that I want you all to understand—just as you mustn't accept a price that is too high, you also must not fight, nor constantly search, for a price that is too low. Our guidelines, which certainly aren't perfect, which can from time to time be reopened for negotiation, are about a fair price. You should be able to afford the things you need in order to live. And you need to understand that those who sell you these things also need to live. You need each other. We need each other. Our guidelines, setting a fair price, will always be about treating each other with a very generous and substantial degree of respect. So we're here to talk about the price of things. But if we're stuck talking about the price of things, we're all really missing the point."

But then the meeting was opened up to the floor and, in fact, swung quite drastically back toward the topic of the price of things. People resumed speaking overtop of one another but slightly less so than before. There were many calculations I found difficult to follow. And I felt sympathy for my translator, who was struggling to translate all the numbers and math. I wanted to tell her she didn't need to bother, I probably wouldn't be able to understand so many rapid-fire monetary calculations anyway, but I also didn't want to undermine the skilled effort she was making to keep everything straight. One thing I do understand, since it's repeated many times over the next several hours, is that prices are meant to remain twenty to thirty per cent cheaper than before liberation. But the guidelines were also vague as to whether any degree of inflation could be included. In principle, there should be no inflation within the system they had created. Inflation is based on a desire for growth, and they weren't aiming for growth, only to meet everyone's needs. But goods smuggled through the fissures in the embargo came from an outside world in which inflation was still very much in play. What's more, people had risked their lives to smuggle things in, so how could one put a price on such a service? Of course one couldn't, but the price should at least take into account the price of things in the world outside of this thin strip of liberated territory. And then how could there be inflation in some things and not others? I wasn't sure if I was understanding any of this correctly. "Most goods that are readily available are produced locally, and to these items the guidelines do apply. Goods from outside are negligible, too few to have any real effect on the general price of things." Huerta was firm on this point. "We need to keep the discussion focused on all the things we make and use together. These are the things that will truly keep us alive and allow us to live." By the end of the meeting she looked exhausted, but nonetheless the translator took me over and introduced us. I said I was impressed by how she held the floor, how clearly she spoke about such complex matters, and the respect everyone seemed to have for her as she spoke. "It's not so complex," she replied. "These are things everyone can understand. That's what I'm always telling people. Everyone can understand the economics of our situation if they fully apply themselves. Actually, that's the main point: for things to work, everyone must also understand *how* they work. If everyone understood that, it would be harder for price-fixers to get away with their dirty little tricks."

Most of the meetings were considerably smaller. I was amazed to see the capacity they all had for talking and trying to figure things out. Meetings with five people around a table talking about what garbage would actually be left if everything that could be composted was, and how to organize for the compost to be used as close as possible to where it was produced, to avoid wasting fuel on transportation. Comparing the ways they reused all plastic, glass, and metal containers. How they planned to keep reusing them basically forever, out of necessity if nothing else, because they didn't yet have the capacity to produce such things. Meetings with twenty people, all of them recent parents, sitting around a preschool trying to figure out what activities would best prepare their very young children for a society that was striving toward more equality than any of them had known at that tender age. If the teachers were unconsciously or unknowingly doing anything to make the boys feel more important than the girls. What assumptions had to be undone to raise their children with a greater sense of equality and possibility. Meetings with forty people, taking place almost in secret and worrying that, already, after only nine years, certain rules were becoming too stratified, and much of the earlier sense of discovery, improvement, and trial and error was too quickly being lost. How to set things in place that need to be set without anything ever becoming too fixed or inflexible. Meetings of around sixty people wondering if, contrary to everything they've been taught and all their known traditions, it would be possible and useful to talk about their sex lives in a public forum such as this one. About twenty minutes into this meeting, a woman points to me, then whispers something to her friend. The friend comes over and asks me to step outside for a moment while they discuss whether everyone present is comfortable having me—an outsider who might very well write about these events—present for the discussion of such an intimate topic. I wait just outside the room for over an hour until the same friend comes out and informs me that they took a vote and it was decided, forty to twenty, that they'd prefer I was not in attendance. She hoped I would understand and, feeling I had no choice, I said I understood. However, I don't think anyone reading this will be surprised to learn it was absolutely the most pure feeling of disappointment I've felt in a very long time.

In one of my previous books I wrote a certain amount about sex. It was by far my most successful book and because of this fact I vowed to never write about sex again. But, of course, much like everywhere, there must be much sex here. Then I think: before this trip, there had never been any violence in my life, but I've never had any qualms writing about violence. Why was I willing to write about violence but not about sex? Because that's the culture I was raised in, having been taught sex was nasty but violence was okay.

Nonetheless, I tried to imagine what they spoke about in that room. Mostly I thought about this while I stood outside waiting to learn whether or not I would be allowed to stay.

For most of that time I felt almost certain I would not be allowed to stay. Why would they possibly want the outside world to know about their sex lives? And I was nothing if not a conduit from the outside world. That must be how many, if not most, of them saw me. I understood there had been previous meetings along these lines that consisted entirely of women, and this was their first attempt at a coed version. My brief survey of the room counted about forty women and twenty men, and I wondered how the vote for my exclusion divided along gender lines. I assumed most of the women voted for putting me out, but was this only a sexist assumption on my part? I assumed that the sexual performance of the men would be brought up and criticized (but why did I assume this?), and therefore maybe it was the men who did not wish to have such information exposed. I wondered what kinds of words they were using: modest words or explicit ones. What would it feel like to stand in front of a room full of people and publicly speak about your sex life for the very first time? (And then I wondered: Had I ever stood in front of a room full of people and spoken about my sex life? I had to admit I had not.) I saw so many inspiring and important things on that thin strip of land and yet this one meeting I did not actually see took on such an oversized importance in my non-memory of it. There was a moment I told myself, or wanted to tell myself, that the actual truth of their revolution lay inside that room I was stranded just outside of. That the way we could tell if their emancipation was or was not actually emancipatory was whether or not their sex lives were improving. But then I realized I was being stupid. I've always wanted to believe that sex was political, and I'm sure there's a certain degree of truth to this position, but I had to step back, see the larger picture, that so many of the other things I was witnessing were, in fact, infinitely more political than anyone's private sex life. Each committee I witnessed was led by one man and one woman, or by two women, but never by a single individual and never by two men; this was an attempt at creating equality that went so far beyond anyone's potential orgasm. Staring at that closed door that I was not allowed to enter, and thinking about the discussion taking place behind it, I realized there was a kind of truth or poetry to my exclusion. And also it was a kind of cliché. At that moment I was living the cliché of the hidden seeming more important simply because it is hidden, and somehow this was also one of the most common and unhelpful clichés for understanding sex.

Once again I stand in front of the target, in front of the old barn that continues to taunt me. Once again I aim and carefully fire. Of course I miss. Goldman hadn't been by to watch me miss for a while. But today, once again, she was there. Maybe she wanted to see if I had improved or maybe she just wanted a good laugh at my expense. If the latter was the case, I did not disappoint. It is amazing to me how much laughter there is here, as if, when you are constantly in danger, when every day might be your last, you want to squeeze in as much laughter as possible. Then again, the one time I did hit the bull's eye she let out an unbelievable cheer, a joyous whooping, like she had been on my side all along, as if I too was a vital part of their ongoing struggle and victory. I could see why she made a good commander: the joy she expressed at the accomplishment of others made you want to excel, to do your best. Why wouldn't I want to hit the target again if it gave another human being such exhilarating pleasure at my minor accomplishment? When my daily allotment of bullets was gone, we once again went for a walk by the river.

"You might think you're not improving but you are," she says. "I can see it."

I smile in acknowledgement, afraid my smile is too sad and I should muster a bit more faith as she continues.

"At any rate, you're obviously not here to shoot. That improvement is only icing on the cake."

"What am I here for?" I ask, surprised at my own question. Surprised how genuinely I want to know her take on my situation. And she doesn't answer right away. We're walking and she's thinking and I'm waiting, hoping that out of nowhere she has some great insight on the matter, an angle that has never occurred to me before. But in the end she only says, "You're here because you have a way with words." The next thing, what happened the next moment, seems wrong to me. Not wrong that it happened but wrong that I should retell it. As if I'm making everything too romantic and adventurous, or romantically stretching the truth. But it would also feel wrong not to include it. We both stop walking. Goldman a few feet ahead of me, completely still. I imitate her, also standing as still as possible. I look at her and all I can think is that she's listening. Then, in one fluid movement, she turns to her left, raises her rifle, fires, and in the distance I can almost see a man, who also appears to be holding a rifle, fall from a tree and hit the ground. "I have a way with aim and you have a way with words," she says. And I laugh. I don't know who the man is or how she knew he was there and for a moment it seems possible the entire incident has been staged solely for my benefit. "I have no proof," she says, "but I've always suspected you can feel when there's a weapon pointed at you. Some sort of animal instinct. You can feel it at the back of your head like a menace. But I think

76

I might have also heard a branch crack. The way a branch cracks under a human foot, it's such a specific sound. And that means it couldn't be one of us. We don't climb trees. That's a sniper move. We fight in self-defence. I'm only telling you all this because you must be curious. Wondering what you just saw. They've tried to kill me a bunch of times, but I swear I have nine lives, and then another nine after that. Still, it's important to pay attention." We make our way over to where I think I saw the man fall but he's long gone. There's a bloodstain on the ground, still damp against the leaves, a whiff of evidence that partially helps convince me I didn't make up the entire thing.

I didn't know if she had really been in danger, if I almost just saw her killed, and realized how sad I would be if anything happened to her. I did feel she was on duty, watching over me, trying to make sure I wasn't a spy or double agent, but she was doing her duty with such kindness. Maybe that was also part of her job, to demonstrate self-defence with a human face.

I press down on the Record button. I hear it click as the tape begins to roll forward:

—We sit in a big circle of chairs. All on the same level. That detail is really important.

—Why is it important?

—It's like the opposite of a normal courtroom. Where the judge is at the podium. If that's what it's called. Where the judge is higher up than everyone else. In the circle we're all on the same level. No one is higher than anyone else.

—But there is still a judge?

—There are facilitators. Most of the time there are more than one. We're working to negotiate a solution. We're working toward justice, but it's a different model. It's recuperative, restorative. We don't believe in punishment. We want to see people realize what they've done wrong, be held accountable by the community, and really begin to change. We want to see people change in deeper ways, so they don't continue to do harm.

—And everything can be dealt with in this way, every kind of complaint?

—Everything except murder. That's another process.

—What happens in the case of a murder?

—It might be better if you speak about that with someone else. Someone who's actually been through that process. I have a wealth of experience. It's better if we talk about things I've actually experienced myself.

—Of course.

—I don't want to be difficult.

—You're not being difficult. What you're saying is reasonable. It's better to talk about things that you know about.

—Yes. Thank you.

—So what happens when you sit in the circle? How do you start?

—The person who has been wronged starts by explaining what happened. From their perspective. During this part the accused shouldn't speak. Or should speak as little as possible. It's important that they sit and really listen to what they've done. Or what they're accused of.

—Are they innocent until proven guilty?

—Yes. But that doesn't matter as much. Because they're not going to be punished. They're most likely not going to be punished until they repeat their behaviour again and again and, because they fail to learn from their mistakes, need to be removed for the good of the community. And then they're moved to a different process. But that happens very rarely, you'd be surprised. What we do in the circle, I mean, we're all going to work together to come to as full an understanding as possible of what happened, from everyone's perspective, and then we're going to try to come to a recuperative arrangement that's satisfying for everyone. It might be as simple as them apologizing and promising never to do it again. And often a significant portion of the community is there, so they know if they do it again it will be noticed and they'll be brought back to the circle. Maybe next time a smaller circle with us and a group of their immediate friends. People they respect and want to keep in their lives. So being guilty, while maybe no one likes it, it's not nearly as scary if it's not connected to punishment.

—What happens next? After the first explanation?

—Others in the circle are invited to tell the story from their own perspective. If there are different versions of the facts, they're compared and discussed. Everyone's perspective is taken into account, but if the majority of people agree on how it happened, that has to be taken very seriously. Then the person accused is given a chance to tell their side of the story. What's especially important is that we come to an understanding of why they did it, that we can understand their reasons, and those reasons must also be listened to. What's really important is people listening to each other and coming to an arrangement about how to proceed. There's not some other level that will take responsibility for making the problem go away. The actual people involved need to find a solution to the problem, in the best-case scenario a solution that everyone agrees with and can live with.

—I suppose people don't always agree.

—We're not looking for absolute agreement. It's not a perfect world. We just have to stay in the circle, or keep coming back to the circle, until some sort of agreement is reached. As I said, there is a higher court. So if it's absolutely impossible to come to an agreement, the dispute can be moved on toward another process. But that's not what anyone wants. It's our job as facilitators to help everyone present understand that our lives will be better if we learn how to live together and find ways to resolve our disputes ourselves.

I was taken to a school. Over the course of the year, I was taken to many schools. So many government and private buildings had been repurposed as schools. This was the School for Free Ideas and Thinking, the one they thought I would be most interested in. The students and teachers all cooked and cleaned together, that was one of the first things they told me about it. But then they told me this was also true of all the other schools. It wasn't unique to the School for Free Ideas and Thinking. Still, it was interesting that this was one of the first things they wanted me to know.

That cleaning and cooking together was their gateway drug to thinking together. That everything was connected. The students built their own curriculum as they went along, and I found myself there during a semester dedicated to questions of communal living and collective child-rearing. From what was conveyed to me via a series of translators, it was one of the most thorough ongoing discussions on any topic I have ever witnessed. I do not feel they came to any conclusions. Rarely did I ever feel they were working toward anything even resembling a conclusion.

I'm fairly certain I was the oldest person in the room. The teachers were ten to fifteen years younger than me and the students at least half my age. I would listen to them discuss and realize they're at an age when everything still feels possible. When I was their age I felt so much more was possible in the world than I feel now and I wonder what happened to me. (Then again, I know I'm just another broken idealist. The greater the youthful idealism, the greater the disillusionment when it's smashed or breaks.) I found myself imagining what it would feel like to be that age and be born into this experiment. You've lived your entire life knowing that tomorrow could be the day you or someone you love is taken by a bomb or bullet. But you've also lived the past nine years surrounded by people who are taking control of their own destiny toward a reality you may or may not understand is unprecedented. For you it's always been like this.

In class, most often, everyone is also sitting in a large circle. It takes me a while to figure out who the teacher is and some days I guess wrong. And I'm asked why it even matters, why it's so important for me to single out a particular participant and designate them "teacher." I don't think it's so important, but I'm here trying to observe and understand what I'm observing. And it's definitely not a free-for-all, there are parameters for these discussions and, at times, it does seem that someone is leading. And there are age differences and differences in experience, though I also have to ask myself to what degree such things really matter. As we get older we learn things through experience, but perhaps there are other, equally important, things we forget along the way, or forget to relearn, or unlearn. They say to me: we're all learning from each other, and this is clearly a fact, there's no need for me to question it. What I'm calling the parameters have a lot to do with ensuring everyone participates equally, that one person doesn't speak more than the others, and if someone is dominating the discussion, you can feel everyone nervously glance at them, wondering how long until they take the hint. I assume there must be a less passive-aggressive way they could enforce these don't-talk-too-much parameters, like with a stopwatch for example, but I also see that this would run counter to the principles of what they're trying to do. They're trying to make it feel natural, to teach themselves through experience and practice how to have group discussions in which all can contribute equally. It's definitely not easy.

How to report these discussions, discussions with so many participants. For better or worse I wasn't recording. I should have written down all their names but didn't. And names haven't especially been the point of all I've written so far. I wish I could be back there now, listening to endless youthful reflections on community and living together with care. But I'm losing my grip on the point. Here is part of what I remember and what I've been able to piece together from my unfortunately rather scattered notes. I wish I could capture more of the feeling of it all, but perhaps what most captures the feeling is how much I wish I was back there now:

"I was raised by one mother and one father. And I think large swaths of my personality come from each of them. But if I had been raised by more people, maybe I would have had more choices, more things to learn from, more examples of how to think and live and be."

"You probably weren't just raised by your parents. I assume you also had aunts and uncles and grandparents. Maybe also neighbours, teachers."

"Yes, but my parents were the main ones. My main examples. I can see it so clearly in myself, how my thinking and personality come from them."

"How would it work? How could you have been raised by more people?"

"Maybe I should let someone else speak. I feel I've already spoken a lot."

"I think it has to do with adults knowing they have to earn the respect of the children. And children having a degree of choice as to what adults they spend the most time with. Or the choice to learn different things from different adults."

"But if there was one adult who let the children eat candy and ice cream for every meal, maybe all the children would gather around only that one."

"I don't think it would take most children very long to

realize that eating candy and ice cream three times a day doesn't make you feel very good."

"When I was a child, it would have taken me many years to learn that lesson."

"We've already agreed there would have to be rules. The question is what kinds of rules can we imagine that would produce the desired results. I don't think 'You're not allowed to feed children only candy and ice cream' would be a controversial rule."

"But children themselves would need to have a say shaping those rules. And maybe some of the children would push for their right to eat only candy and ice cream."

"I want us to get back to the main point. What we're talking about is not a society in which children can simply do what they want. We're talking about a world in which children can be raised and influenced—can learn from—a greater array of adult experiences and perspectives. Where children aren't trapped mainly in the world of only two adults."

"To what extent would the mother and father still be the main force in the child's life?"

"That's the question that's so hard to answer."

"It could be different for different children. Maybe some children would gravitate more toward their parents and others would gravitate more toward a larger community. But you can see how this would encourage a parent to work to earn the respect of their child."

"If I were a mother and my child 'gravitated toward a larger community,' I think I would find it extremely hurtful. These are also people's feelings we're talking about."

"But maybe this could also change: that mother could instead feel happy and proud that her child is getting all the knowledge and stimulation they need to thrive. It's not only the children who will be changed by these proposals. The adults would be changed as well."

"I think if we talk about something very simple—like large, daily communal meals—we could see that these proposals aren't even particularly radical. Everyone eats together. Everyone cooks and cleans up together. Children included. The children get to meet and talk to all the different adults and also to play with all the other children. And eating together is a way of coming together, of building community. Even if this happened just once a week, I think you would start to see its effects. It could happen at the level of the neighbourhood, like so many of the developments we've seen."

"I hope we're talking about more than communal meals."

"It could be a start."

"Where does it lead? Isn't that what we're here to imagine? To think about? To ask ourselves?"

"This makes me think that too much choice can be confusing. It would be important not to give the children too many choices. Not to overwhelm them."

"Every time someone says 'the children,' I feel confused. I

mean, weren't we all children once, actually not so long ago? Aren't *we* 'the children'? Shouldn't we be thinking about what *we* would have wanted and needed at their age?"

"It's not only a question of children having more input and influences. It's also a question of a greater number of adults taking responsibility for the raising of children, of collectivizing the tasks that can most easily be made more collective."

"That reminds me of the first thing I thought when we started in on this topic. That parenting is hard and we should be searching for ways to make it easier. To make it feel better. Also that parenting makes you feel more disconnected from the rest of the community because you're so focused on all the things you need to do to make sure your children survive, and we should be searching for ways to counterbalance that."

"But no one is going to care about a child more than the parent. Do we really think that direct link of parental care should be decentred?"

"Is it really so impossible to imagine a society in which all adults care about all children to the same degree?"

"I actually think it might be."

"It sounds like we're saying children have more to learn from adults than they do from other children. And I don't think that's true. They have just as much or more to learn from the other children."

"I don't think anyone here is going to disagree with that."

"I notice we haven't been talking about school. About the adult encounters the child has with their teachers at school."

"Abolish all schools except this one."

"That's the kind of self-defeating joke I hope the next generation of children won't feel nearly as compelled to make or laugh at. But since I'm from this generation, I want to say on the record: I find it funny."

"We need schools where instead of teaching you a series of questionable skills and facts, they actually teach you how to live. But maybe the word for such a place, or such an idea, can't quite be the word *school*."

Later I was asked to teach writing to young people. I said no, I didn't really feel comfortable doing that. I didn't think I was especially qualified. I was told in response that I was their guest, they had shown me enormous hospitality, and the least I could do was repay it by spending a few days of my time teaching. I had basically never taught before and the few times I had tried it hadn't gone so well. It wasn't clear to me what exactly it was that made me a bad teacher, but nonetheless I knew it was true. But I wasn't going to say no (or, at least, I wasn't going to say no twice). So early one morning I found myself in front of a room full of teenagers who allegedly all had an interest in writing or in becoming writers. As befits my considerable lack of experience, I didn't know how to start, and I stood in front of the class for considerably too long simply watching them all, wondering what I could say that might be helpful, helpful in terms of improving their writing, or in their understanding of what it means to write, or for that matter in any other way. Because I don't know what else to do, I say: "Maybe I could just start by taking a few questions. It might help me know a little bit about where you're all at with writing and life. Feel free to ask me anything." And then what followed felt like one of the longest, most spiritually empty group silences I have experienced in my life. But it probably wasn't all that long. I don't know what I was expecting, except that I must have been expecting the worst: Awkward question after awkward question, all of which I was at a complete loss to answer. I remember someone once told me, or maybe I read it, that the secret to being a good teacher was to be genuinely interested in what the students have to say. So as the silence ebbed and flowed, I tried to focus on being genuinely interested, until finally a student in the front row let me off the hook by raising their hand as things, in fits and starts, began to unfold.

Question: Why do you write?

—I'm not sure I understand.

—Why do you write? Does it make you feel good? Do you do it for the money?

At "Do you do it for the money?" many in the room begin to laugh. And in their laughter I could already tell they understood writing, that there was something a little bit absurd or pathetic about it, perhaps the word I'm really searching for is *ineffective*. At least, I think they understood that. I might be projecting. They might have simply been laughing at me in the same way students have always laughed at teachers since the beginning of time. Or at least since the beginning of education. And I believe students should laugh at their teachers, so I tried to enjoy it, although it's certainly difficult to truly enjoy laughter when it's directed mockingly at oneself.

My answer: I don't know. I started writing when I was so young. I didn't have many friends. (More laughter.) But I'm not really sure I even wanted friends. What I really liked was to read. And if I really liked reading what other people had written, maybe in the future others might, in the same way, like my writing. So I think that's how it started. Does that answer your question?

There was more awkward silence. I wondered if this was what I was here for. To try to explain myself to teenagers I would probably never see again. I wondered if I should give them writing exercises and if I could actually think of any, or if I was able to make some up on the spot, off the top of my head. This was a far cry from the School for Free Ideas and Thinking. There they had (almost) no teachers and I worried the problem now was I was taking up too much space in the role of the teacher, in the role of the foreign expert, blocking whatever engagement might otherwise be happening between them in their youthful excitement around the idea of writing. And then I realized what I must have already known from before I arrived: My art is not what they need here. They need their own art. If I could tell them anything I should try to tell them that. As if they didn't already know. Can I tell them they have more to learn from each other than they do from me? That learning from each other might give needed density to their shared experience? Or if I tell them, does it ruin it? Ruin the experience of discovering it for themselves? I could tell my discomfort was making the rest of the room even more uncomfortable, until a student in the third row rescued me with a second question and slowly, finally, things began to get rolling.

Question: Do you need to know how the story will end when you sit down to start it?

My answer: Probably there are writers who work that way. But that's never been my approach. I see it more like life, or like a good conversation. In life you can never be sure what will happen. In a good conversation you never know what the other person will say. I try to start writing each day with that same openness. Does that answer your question?

I now realized I had been wrong, things weren't rolling at all, as another long, empty silence continued to assure me. Did I really start writing without any idea where it would lead? Or was this only a lie I told myself in order to... For what reason exactly? In order to make myself feel or seem more spontaneous, alive, and free than I actually am. Knowing how something ends means there's no reason to set out in the first place. That's what I find so overwhelmingly exciting about being here, wondering how it will evolve, what will happen, what choices they will continue to make, and where those choices will lead. And yet the cynic in me feels I already know where it will lead. Sooner or later one of the surrounding countries, most likely with the covert or not so covert backing of my government, will bomb it and bomb it and bomb it again until there's absolutely nothing left of their fragile, emancipatory experiment. But I don't want to say that or even think it for fear it will become a self-fulfilling prophecy. And I have been wrong about so many things before. And I certainly don't want to say anything like that to this room full of snarky yet clearly still hopeful teenagers. Right now there is something happening that gives them a chance to fully live. Even if it's short-lived, it's an opportunity they shouldn't miss. Is there anything I can say that might help them realize this? I am once again rescued from this unresolved question by a different question from the back row, asked so quietly that at first I don't understand, so they need to repeat it twice before I fully hear them.

Question: Do you think we should be writing in our own language or in yours?

I start answering too quickly, then stop myself. I was about to say that of course they should be writing in their own language. But was that true or so obvious? It's like I was about to suggest they begin to build their own national literature, and yet everyone I've met here insists they are not trying to build yet another nation-state. (And wasn't I filled with hatred for my own country's mediocre, individualistic attempt at creating a national literature?) Here they were searching for another model: more free and open and considerably less defined. How to rule not with power but against power. They would implement certain aspects of the nation-state in order to more fully interact with the rest of the world. But they would attempt to do so without ever fully becoming an actual nation-state. So were these young people writing for each other or, to put it a little stupidly, were they writing for me?

My answer: Now I think you've got me. You've asked a truly difficult question. And my answer will probably say more about me than it will about anything you should or shouldn't do. Because what does it matter what I think? What you write, and whatever language you write it in, needs to come from your own burning analysis of the situation. Does that answer your question?

When they replied, they were speaking louder, I could now

clearly hear them, clearly hear that my answer had not in any way pleased them.

—No, that doesn't answer my question at all. I already know that, in the end, I have to decide what I'm going to do. I want to know what *you* think. I've lived here my entire life. You've lived in other places. Your language is my second language, and I'm good enough but have a less than perfect grasp of it. You actually have more information as to what it would mean for me to write in it. What, if anything, it would give me greater access to. Do you understand what I'm asking?

I did understand but didn't know the answer. It was a question about power. For so many awful and historical reasons, one language has more power than another. So do you choose the language with more power or the one with less? And as I thought this, I had to ask myself again, though I had already asked myself the question so many times, what was my relationship to these people and their struggle? Then I remembered something I couldn't believe I had already forgotten. I didn't even know if it was true: the secret to being a good teacher is being genuinely interested in what the students have to say.

My second attempt at an answer: The thing is, we both have experiences that the other one doesn't have. You have the feeling of living here, of being completely part of this experiment, which I'll never know. I've never been completely a part of anything.

—You're romanticizing me. You think I'm the perfect young revolutionary. But I'm a wannabe writer just like you. (More laughter.) That's why I'm here. So as one wannabe to another, as a young wannabe from here to an old wannabe from there, what would you think if you read an account written by someone like me, but it was written in your language?

My third attempt at an answer: If I'm honest, it takes me to a place I'm not proud of. The real answer is that it wouldn't make me think anything. I wouldn't even notice what language you're writing in. To my eternal shame I'm unilingual. I've failed to learn any other languages. I remember once being told: "It must be terrible not to have a secret language." They meant that when they were outside their own country, in public spaces, they could speak to their friends in their own language and be fairly confident those around them would not eavesdrop or understand. So you have one language you can use mainly to speak with each other and another language for speaking to people like me. And you get to choose. If you write in your own language, I most likely won't see or read it. You can use your own language, in fiction or nonfiction, to plot against me or more fully understand your own situation. At least, that's how it seems to me, but I don't really know, because I'll never experience anything like that. I'm only speculating. But every time I answer this question I feel I'm missing the point — that there's something really important happening here, all around you, and if you have the desire to write about it you should write about it now, as it's happening, because there's no one else in the world who can do so but you.

I felt that maybe this landed, but it was hard to tell. And then I wondered if it was true for so many other things as well. Moments when each of us experience something that will happen only once and we shouldn't miss it, to fully live we must pay attention, catch the wave while it's cresting.

But already this sounded to me like a bad self-help book. And I believed, felt, that what they were experiencing here was almost the opposite of a self-help book, because it was so collective, because they were experiencing it so much together.

Question: This isn't really a question. But it seems to me that you make everything really complicated. Do all writers do that?

I didn't know what to say. I didn't know if all writers made things so complicated. Certainly some writers did. Just like some people in all walks of life. And I had to admit that I was one of them and that it didn't always serve my best interests as a writer or as a person. I think there was more, but you get the idea. Once again I wasn't recording, but I can assure you it all went a bit like that.

The hardest month was the month I spent working on the farm. Except for the day Zana came to visit. I said before that I had never taught, but obviously I had far more experience in front of a classroom than I did working the fields. They did their best to train me, but I fear by the end of the first week they gave up and let me do my allotted tasks as slowly and poorly as I could. (Which, for me, felt like doing them as quickly and as well as possible.) I harvested tomatoes, eggplants, mushrooms, and oranges. I carefully packed tomatoes, eggplants, mushrooms, and oranges into large wooden boxes. I fed pigs, ducks, and cattle, who were all allowed to roam freely and had their run of the place. I sprayed crops with a pesticide-free naturopathic liquid that smelled a bit like cinnamon. It didn't smell just like cinnamon, but I could never figure out exactly what that scent reminded me of. The liquid seemed to work. In my non-expert opinion, even over the course of a month I could see and feel the crops responding. They rotated my tasks so I got a chance to experience how everything worked. At the end of each day I was so exhausted I could barely move. I wouldn't attempt to guess how many people reading this have worked on a farm, even for a day, and how many have never worked on a farm. I'm sure many who have worked on a farm were considerably more suited for it than I was, which of course wouldn't be difficult.

I knew Zana had arrived because I heard her laughing. (I've seen the revolution and it laughed at me.) I was bent over in the dirt, pulling something out of the ground, maybe carrots, I no longer remember, and I looked over to see Zana laughing. I knew she was coming but had forgotten this was the day. Working every day, I'd lost track of the days of the week. I now thought of the days of the week more in terms of which tasks I was expected to do, tasks that were written on a sheet of paper and slid under my door at the beginning of the week. (It was done this way so the one person here who spoke my language could translate instructions from several people and then convey them to me all at once, as clearly as possible. The system was efficient, if a bit impersonal. I always found the instructions exceedingly clear.) I washed my hands and face from a basin I filled from the well and we went to the kitchen to drink tea. Zana apologized for laughing but said the sight of me crouched over in the fields was the funniest thing she had ever seen, at which point she starts laughing again and can't stop. I drink my tea and watch her laugh. When her laughter finally subsides, we get to talking, and she asks how it feels for me, this life of working on a farm, how it feels for a person who so clearly isn't suited or accustomed to it. I start to answer, then stop myself, wanting to take a moment first to think about what I've learned here. From day to day I was so exhausted I didn't even realize I was learning. But when she asked the question, my understanding shifted, and I thought maybe I was. Also, didn't I come here to learn? I understood the things I was doing here each day had a lot to do with helping and a lot to do with getting out of the way. And there was a sense in which both helping and getting out of the way could be seen on a continuum. The point was for nature to replenish itself, in cycles, with the seasons. You could help this happen and then you could get out of the way and allow it to continue. The idea I found so potent was that it was possible to set processes in motion that would replenish the soil, a shift from something dying toward that same thing soon thriving. I wanted to see this as a metaphor for everything else but didn't really know if it could serve as a metaphor. If humans went away, nature would thrive. But if nature went away, humans would definitely not thrive. Nonetheless, I was here to try to convince myself that humans were not, in and of themselves, the problem. That humans could organize differently and in doing so create new possibilities. Wasn't that what I had been seeing and hearing?

I said to Zana: "I wonder if I could just drop everything. If I could spend the rest of my life working on this farm. If they would have me. What it would be like and what it would do."

Zana said: "You'd be miserable. Even I can see that."

I said: "I'm already miserable. Maybe it's time for me to be miserable in a completely different way."

Zana said: "Are you seriously considering this? Or is it just more of your aimless intellectual speculation?"

I could tell she already knew the answer. I constantly had the feeling that everyone I interacted with here had spoken with each other, spoken about me behind my back, and together they had formed a fairly accurate portrait of my character. But maybe I was being paranoid. Or maybe I was an open book. You didn't have to spend much time with me before you basically got it, were able to assess my character with a fair degree of accuracy. And yet wasn't I changing?

I said: "The way the animals roam free gives me such a good feeling. Watching them hunting for insects, at their own pace, coming in and out of view as I work."

Zana said: "You make it sound like a petting zoo."

I said: "Why is that bad?"

Zana said: "Last month a pig wandered onto a land mine and exploded."

I laughed and thought, in a few moments, Zana would begin laughing along with me, but she did not. Her demeanour made it clear she didn't particularly care for the way I was laughing. I wondered if she was sad the pig was killed, but felt almost certain it couldn't be that. This was their revolution, not a petting zoo. This was their revolution and she clearly didn't like hearing it compared to something cute.

Zana continued: "Pigs are smart animals. It looks like the other pigs have already learned from the first pig's mistake. So we don't think it will happen again. In permaculture they like to say 'the problem is the solution,' meaning that by examining any given problem you can begin to find your way through it. We can regenerate the soil over time but

97

not if they keep bombing it. Most of the time I try not to think that way. The problem might be the solution, but here we're actually turning the proverb inside out. Or sideways. More like the solution is both the problem and the solution. If people are happy on this thin strip of land, if the food is good and the soil keeps growing it, and if everyone knows about this happiness, they will want to stop fighting and live like this instead. When I talk to soldiers from the other sides, when I clearly explain our project to them, I can sometimes feel it in their voices. They want to move here, give it a try. And some of them do. We can't end this war by fighting it. We need to end war by proving there's another way for people to live together. By proving it's what most people actually want. If we design it properly, even if all the people here were to die, every last one, this farm would continue bearing fruit and crops, and keeping the animals alive, for at least another three hundred years. Those are the kinds of time periods we really need to think in. Seven generations into the future and all that. Now every day our lives feel in danger, but three hundred years from now, if we can hang on long enough, until the surrounding conflicts subside, who knows what might be possible. I'm not sure exactly how, but we need to be thinking that far into the future. Watching more and more things be able to grow here each year, you start to get a sense of how far into the future this project might stretch. You're really just a tourist here."

I start to object, but she interrupts me.

"You don't see any problem with being a tourist because you don't actually know anything else. No offence, but it seems to me you're mostly even a tourist in your own life. A tourist won't stick it out with us even through our immediate short-term difficulties, much less work hard to prepare the way for the next three hundred years. We're not asking you for that kind of commitment. But even if you just get a taste of it, you might have something to take back home with you and then later tell the world. Tell the world to stop bombing us so we can begin to create this beautiful place that might even last for another three hundred years. That's why I recommended you to work on this farm. Because I wanted you to get a taste of it, of one possible future. Do you think you did?"

I was listening, but at the same time my mind was drifting off, back toward these past few weeks of farming. It was true that if I dedicated my life to farming I would be miserable, in a very different way than if I simply continued to dedicate my life to writing. What kinds of sacrifices was I willing to make? I didn't know if it was true that I was a tourist, but if it was, perhaps the reason had to do with being a writer, that I visit life only, or mainly, so I can write about it later. Others have made such observations in the past, most likely stated more elegantly and with greater tormented conviction. I tried to bring my mind back to our conversation, so it could focus on Zana's question. So I could answer it. Did I, during these days of working on this farm, get a taste of one possible future? This book isn't reality.

After Zana left, I went back to my work with the plants, animals, and soil. I can't remember for exactly how many more days, I think it was close to another week. And yet now the work felt different; after her visit, after our conversation—which I soon began recalling as her monologue—I felt myself more actively trying to connect the tasks I was given each day to some larger sense of purpose. Most of the time I was working alone, though there were other times I worked in a small group, and on this particular day it was one of the rare occasions there were only the two of us. I don't remember exactly why, or if there was even a reason for this state of affairs, but that's how it was. What I do remember is my partner basically didn't speak a single word of my language and therefore communication was difficult. But also there was something peaceful about how we were working together in silence. Without saying a word, we managed to establish a natural rhythm. He handed me the necessary things and I arranged them, and then later I handed him the necessary things and he arranged them. We worked like this in silence for many hours, but that is not the reason I have such an intense memory of this particular day. The reason is that, at a moment, everything went black. I'm not sure if it happened all at once or if I simply didn't notice it at first because I wasn't paying enough attention. But everything went black and I could feel a sense of animal panic rising within me. I thought maybe we were being bombed or the world was ending in some other unexpected way, until seconds later it occurred to me that what we were experiencing was simply a solar eclipse. (I still don't know for a fact that it was an eclipse. Maybe there was another explanation that didn't occur to me at the time and still hasn't occurred to me.) What I did know, or thought I knew, was that if you were to experience a solar eclipse you should not look up, not stare directly into the eclipsing sun, so I did not look up, instead I looked straight ahead into the temporary darkness and thought about how there must have been eclipses since the beginning of time and how they would continue to occur well into the indefinite future. Wars would come and go, but on some regular rhythm and schedule the moon would occasionally float past and cover the sun, as it had always done. And then my companion, my co-worker, began to sing. It was only much later I realized he must have been singing because he could feel I was starting to panic, and was searching for ways to calm me. Like singing a lullaby to a baby. In the moment all I felt was darkness and his song—a song I imagined as common to the region, but nonetheless, for me, completely new and startling—as it hit me with the full force of an epiphany. I have always loved music. Sometimes I think I have loved music too much. And therefore listening to him sing as we stood there in the darkness was the first time in a very long time, if not ever, that I felt perfectly all right in the world. Maybe that was all the epiphany consisted of. That in this world of injustice and killing and poverty, it was still possible, if only for a moment, to feel okay. And it always had been and always would be. I don't want to make it sound like this was random. It was his voice that did it to me. The actual sung qualities of his voice that seized the moment of darkness to provide, for me, and perhaps for him as well, an experience of pure grace. He knew what he was doing. I could hear it in the way he sang. He closed his eyes and sang as humanely and directly as he knew how. Then, as quickly as the darkness fell, the light also returned. But I don't think it makes sense to speak of anything being either quick or slow. Time bent, flapped, and stuttered as he sang, and I have absolutely no idea for how long we stood there in the darkness, for how long he sang to me, perhaps trying to calm his premonition of my rising panic. Now that I try to remember it more clearly, it's possible I also heard other voices in the distance, also singing the same song or some other song, but this might only be unnecessary elaboration caused by the strain of memory. It felt to me there were other voices singing. Somewhere else, not too far. I couldn't be certain, and still can't. The idea that there were many voices is clearly an idea I find entrancing, almost important. I'm not sure why that would make the memory more consequent. As the light returned, he gradually stopped his singing, faded out, smiled at me as I smiled back, hoping my smile was enough to properly thank him.

I press down the Record button, and we can both hear the tape begin to whir, the now familiar sound of a wheel turning another wheel:

—You come here and, like everyone else, you see women with guns, find it fascinating and think you have to write about it. But the guns are the least interesting aspect of living here.

—Then what's interesting?

—What's important is building something you care about, building something you want to protect. The methods you use to protect it, though necessary, are considerably less interesting.

—I didn't come here because I was interested in guns.

—No, you came because you wanted to see how we're living. How we organize ourselves.

—Yes.

—I won't lie. There are many things I found extremely difficult. Especially at first, closer to the beginning. I'm afraid, like many men of my generation I had fairly backwards ideas when it came to the topic of women. And I've always thought of myself as progressive. Extremely progressive.

But I had to learn the hard way that I wasn't as progressive as I thought.

—Can you give me an example?

—I fear the examples are all clichés. I mean, I find them embarrassing now. Because I've changed, not as much as I'd like to—I still hope to change considerably more in the future. But I have changed, and when I look back at my earlier self I'm embarrassed that I could have been so selfish and so limited. Really clichéd and obvious things: like becoming defensive if I felt a woman had a better idea than me, and instead of getting behind her idea and supporting it, I was wasting my energy, spending all my time searching for reasons why her idea wouldn't work and we should use my idea instead. It's really just ego, stupid male ego, and I hope I don't still do things like that, though sometimes I catch myself, I fear that I do. The ego is powerful, and old habits—the habits we learned as children—they really don't leave us so easily. And then even more basic things: not wanting to cook, not wanting to look after our children as an equal partner. Feeling I would be less of a person if I spent my time cooking and co-parenting. And the strange thing is I really love to cook. I've always loved it. But, I suppose, these are insecurities I learned from my father, through unconscious observation, and he learned from his father and so on; who knows how far back it really goes. But as I said, I guess I just have to keep saying it in order to try to convince myself, I hope I've changed and that I'll continue to change. Because positive change comes through listening, through really hearing what other people say, really considering it, and then changing one's actions accordingly. So what I try to do, what I tell myself I need to keep doing, is really listen. Really listen to what the women in my life, and in our community, are telling me.

—How do you think other men you know, other men who live here, are changing or not changing? Do you have any sense of it? How everyone is dealing with this experiment?

—It's difficult. It's really difficult to say. Every person, every case, is different. I get nervous when I start to generalize. It's clearly possible to say there are a lot of men who haven't changed at all. But how many exactly? And even when you're stubborn and you don't want to change, when the world is changing around you, there's a way in which you can't help it. It changes you anyway. At least, that's what I think. When everything is changing around you, you change as well, though not always for the better.

—What do you mean? How does it change people for the worse?

—Some men double down on their previous convictions. Become more macho or less open. I've seen it happen. But I really don't want to dwell on that. I believe it was suggested you interview me because I'm one of the good ones, because I'm trying to be very open about a struggle that maybe a lot of men here are living more in secret. And I just think it's really important that we talk about it, as much as possible. That we don't let our fragile male egos lead us into the trap of unnecessary resentment. Because when you talk about it, the first thing you learn is that a lot of people are experiencing the exact same thing as you. You're not alone. Thinking you're alone, that you are the only one in the world who feels this way, is one of the easiest ways to resist change.

—How do you envision this new situation you find yourself in? How do you understand it?

—It's strange...five or six years ago I didn't even know what "structural inequality" was. I'd never heard of it, had no language or way of understanding what it was. But when you start to understand it a bit, well...the first thing you begin to understand is that it's all so much larger than you. You can change your behaviour, but unless larger, more structural things also begin to change, the problems will keep coming back, generation after generation. And what does it really mean to change these larger structures? Mainly it means changing the rules, the rules we all agree to live by. These rules can take the form of laws, but also of stories, conventions, and social customs. And it all has to eventually change and really we're at the very beginning.

The tape runs out. I hear the click of the button popping up from the recorder. It was my last tape. For everything else that was going to happen to me here, I would have to rely solely on my memory. There would be no further recordings to assist in the process. After the interview, I found myself wondering once again, asking myself: Had I changed as well and really how much? If I were to stay here forever, never return home, never write or publish this book, would that create the conditions for even further change? Would I change more here than I would at home, if I were to fully commit myself to this struggle? It was not my struggle, but maybe it could become so over time.

It was at least ten months of living as a temporary guest on this thin strip of land before I was finally allowed to throw my rifle over my shoulder and join them on patrol. On patrol with me were Goldman, Zana, and Huerta. There were several others out with us as well. I unfortunately didn't learn their names. I interacted mainly with those I had already interacted with before. I don't think it was a coincidence that Goldman, Zana, and Huerta were with me on patrol. I think they had been assigned to me. The terrain was rough, rougher than I had expected, and I had to struggle to keep up. I'm not sure how it arose, but at one point they all began questioning me about my journey here. How did I get here? How did I find it? Which direction had I come from? How and why did I begin the journey? And then very suddenly Zana got a strange look on her face, some new and perplexing thought having only now occurred to her, and she said: "But how did you avoid the land mines?"

I said: "There were land mines?"

What I said was then translated for all of the others, and I've never seen a group of women laugh so hard in my life. They just kept laughing and laughing and it seemed to go on endlessly. Apparently the area I had walked across to get here was drenched in land mines, and the fact that I didn't step on one and blow myself up was nothing short of a miracle. How did I survive, wandering my way through the land mines? Was it simply luck? Pure and uncanny luck? This book isn't reality. Goldman then explained to me that there would be no land mines over the area we would be covering on patrol. That with great effort, and at the cost of several lives, they had now all been cleared.

As we slowly rounded our way up toward the top of a—for me, painfully steep—embankment, I could feel how out of breath I was. None of the others appeared to be struggling. With each step I took, I feared I would slip, lose my footing, sprain an ankle, or some other muck-up my neurosis could not yet anticipate. It was amazing, but not surprising, how routine it all seemed for the others, compared to how nerve-racking I found the terrain. And I wasn't even considering the possibility we might be attacked at any moment. This stress was the same stress I might have felt taking a hike or mountain climbing. It was not the stress of war. We were surrounded by war, but I was merely struggling with the physical exercise of an extended hike through a challenging landscape. To distract myself, I asked Goldman, really just trying to think of something to say, if she had always been so good with a gun—for example, ever since childhood—and if she genuinely saw any possibility that my marksmanship might eventually improve.

Goldman: If you want it badly enough, trust me, you'll improve. Or if your life depends on it.

Me: If my life depends on it, it might already be too late.

Goldman: That's the madness of the matter. You'll either surprise yourself or you won't. All that practice will have been worth it or not.

I thought: Here I am. Finally out on patrol with them. Since I arrived here, it now seemed to me, I've wanted this, though now that it's happening I can't possibly imagine why, what it represented for me or what I thought it would be like. Putting my life on the line, albeit in a routine and not especially dangerous manner, alongside these women I've come to admire so much, felt like both the least I could do and the most important thing.

Me: You spoke to me before about how it might be different

for a woman to kill than for a man...

Goldman apparently didn't like where this was headed and was already interrupting me: Look, what we're doing here, what's important, it's not just because we're women with guns. Before you leave here, you really must understand that. It's because we're women with guns putting our thinking and will and energy toward a truly emancipatory project. Working together with men and each other and anyone else who genuinely wants to make it happen. I live for the day when everyone joins us and we won't need any of these guns anymore. That would be a truly worthwhile goal.

Zana: We don't even have good guns.

Goldman: The guns we have are really shit.

Me: Why don't you have good guns?

Huerta: The embargo.

Me: Tell me about the embargo.

Huerta: I don't know. Maybe the embargo is even helpful. It forces us to rely on ourselves, to work with what we have.

Goldman: We can grow our own food but we can't make our own guns.

It was working, the conversation was taking my mind off of how out of breath I was. I kept reminding myself that this was only a routine patrol, that they did this every single day, that my struggle to keep up was analogous to my struggle to keep up in all the other ways.

Zana: We do have *some* good guns.

Goldman: Too few.

Me: Where do they come from?

Huerta: You get three guesses and the first two don't count.

I realized they were the guns from dead enemy soldiers. I had already been told about this but had momentarily forgotten. Fighting an enemy that had better weapons than you did. Isn't that what we were always doing? And sometimes you could take a few, but the enemy would have more. We were now weaving along a path with steep hills on either side of us. The others had all begun to slow down and it was clear they were only doing so to make the patrol a little easier on me. I was slowing them down despite my best efforts to keep up. But what did it matter if you went on patrol quickly or more slowly—was speed really the point?

Huerta: The embargo colours everything. How we live, everything we have or don't have, in one way or another can be brought back to those restrictions. It's like running a marathon with your hands tied behind your back. But the amazing thing—at least, this is what I try to tell myself, try to keep reminding myself—is that we're still in the race. We're still running the marathon.

Zana: I like your idea of the embargo being useful. I think we could even take it further: The embargo, we might say, against its will or against its stated purpose, is teaching us how to live. That you actually don't need so much to live a good life, you probably need quite a bit less than you previously thought. And figuring out your own solutions is a pleasure. We've had to figure out so many things for ourselves because of that fucking embargo. But every time you find a solution there's this sense of accomplishment that couldn't be achieved in any other way.

There was a moment of silence as we rounded the bend and the gunfire started, gunfire from all sides, as we all started running, back in the direction from which we came, taking cover behind some mud and rubbish, a wall that had once been part of a now-destroyed building. I hadn't even noticed it before, when we walked past it a few moments ago, and couldn't understand how we had found it so quickly. We had walked into an ambush and were under attack. The others took turns firing over the wall as we quickly discussed our plan of action, mostly in their language I didn't understand, with occasional snippets translated for me. The consensus was apparently that they had us surrounded, cornered, and things didn't look good. I don't know what came over me, but I loudly made a suggestion. It was the loudest I had spoken since I arrived and therefore they all paused to hear what I had to say, even as they continued to take turns firing over the wall. I would run out into the open and cause a distraction. I would fire at the enemy as often as I could, drawing their fire toward me, away from the rest of the group, allowing the others to escape. I expected them to try to talk me out of it but instead they said: Thank you, that's the best possible solution in our current situation. Perhaps they thought my fellow countrymen wouldn't shoot at me, but I had already learned this was not even remotely true. They handed me two machine guns, weapons I had never actually fired before, explaining that if I remain mostly hidden behind the far ridge, which they then point out to me, and fire both weapons at once, at times also alternating them, I will appear to be a larger group than just one, and it is quite plausible this will draw enemy fire away from the main group. I am normally not brave. Normally I'm even afraid to be out in the rain without an umbrella. But I had stupidly offered, and they had accepted my offer, so there was no backing down now. They quickly showed me how to use the machine guns, once again pointed out the route they thought I should take, and then, suddenly, it was now or never. I scrambled up over the wall and made a beeline for the ridge, running with everything I was worth, finding the other side of the ridge and continuing to run for my life. Each time I pressed down the trigger, the machine gun shook my entire body, as if I was going to die simply from the force of the vibrations. So much adrenaline was surging through my body I felt I could fly, that I was about to achieve liftoff, that these two machine guns could become my wings. As I ran and fired, I wondered if it was working. I could hear the enemy fire but could not tell if it was directed toward me or back at the others. I looked over my shoulder, but the past was a blur. And then I turned, and the future shook into sudden sharp relief. Up ahead was a plane coming straight at me. It had clearly spotted me and was already swooping down for a better look. I froze in my tracks and stared up at the plane, staring it down. Everything speeding forward, I could feel each millisecond passing me by. It must have only been the adrenaline that was responsible for my sudden surge of hopeful or wishful thinking, but in that moment I absolutely expected the plane to explode in the air above me. It happened before and it would now happen again. I stood in place, waiting for the plane to explode. But the plane did not explode. I gaze up at the bomb as it is released. The bomb is falling directly toward me. It is over. I can see it homing in. My last thought before the hit: Am I dying for a cause? Did I live for one?

Interlude

When you're reading a book, you can put it down and pick it up again. You have a bookmark to hold your place. In life, if you're lucky and privileged, you can go away, take a vacation, then return back to your normal life, picking it up more or less where you left off. Even in wartime there are occasional stories, both sides laying down their guns and playing soccer together for a while, before the battle resumes. Can there be a novel where the protagonist, the narrator, dies halfway through? What kind of novel would that be? A bomb kills indiscriminately. It doesn't care if you're the protagonist or some minor character. And we're all protagonists in our own lives.

Something I don't particularly like about this book I'm writing is how focused it is on a single narrator. I've always wanted to write novels of collectivity, but have so far never managed to do so. I think much of the reason for this inability has to do with the fact that I was raised in this culture, with its overemphasis on individualism, just like almost everyone else I know. Wanting to escape it, by itself, does only a fraction of the job. When I was young, I remember going to an anarchist meeting in which someone said: We were all raised in a sexist, racist culture. Therefore, it is impossible for any of us to not be sexist and racist, we all grew up in this culture and we all have a great deal of these things inside us. However, it is possible for us to be anti-sexist and anti-racist, to become conscious and fight against these things within ourselves and out in the world. I heard this when I was about seventeen and it's still more or less what I believe today. I suppose, in good literary fiction, the author isn't supposed to break the fourth wall and speak directly to the reader. But I've never completely understood why not.

With this interlude, I'm mainly playing for time, because I honestly can't decide whether or not our narrator, or protagonist, dies. A part of me feels this death is the right choice, the most radical artistic move. The protagonist dies, and for the rest of the book we just see the lives of the other characters. (Is it possible to write about my own death as if it were also the death of capitalism and patriarchy? Unfortunately, capitalism and patriarchy don't die so easily. You kill them and they keep coming back.) But another part of me feels that by dying, I let myself off the hook. Art and politics never work together to the degree to which I dream they might. This book is not reality. When I was in my twenties I heard a musician speak about his pacifism. He said that often when he says he's a pacifist, the reply is: Come on, if someone beat up your mother you'd want to kick their ass. And his reply to this was: Yes, if someone beat up my mother, of course I'd want to kick their ass. Because sometimes violence is necessary, especially in self-defence. (And a revolutionary struggle is also a kind of self-defence.) But the point he wants to make is that, even though it is sometimes necessary, that doesn't make it right, doesn't make it good. Violence is sometimes necessary but it is never good. A bomb doesn't know good from bad, it falls and explodes and kills. And every time it does, someone profits. Someone makes money.

When those soldiers in the real-life fairy tale put down their guns for an afternoon and, instead of fighting, play soccer, they reveal the flip side of war that the logic of constant bombings annihilates. The bombs and missiles and warplanes aren't going to be playing soccer with each other any time soon. I fear I'm just playing for time. This is an anti-war novel in which no one dies, but do I make an exception for our protagonist? Why is his life worth more than that of the others? A novel must have a protagonist, must play its part in celebrating Western culture's overemphasis on the individual. This novel also plays its part, but it is not reality. I've always had the hardest time making decisions.

3: Desire Without Expectation

I wake up in a small white room that I intuitively know is a prison cell. I am atheist to the bone—well, not to the bone since there must also be at least a modicum of spirituality, some spiritual component, to my world view—but if I had been a believer in any of the religions that prescribe hell as an antidote for a badly lived life, I might have believed I had died and this small white room was the hell I'd woken up in. Later I'm told the bomb landed not on me but beside me, close but far enough away. The blast knocked me unconscious. Sent me flying to a spot where, after a long and irritating search, they found me still unconscious, making it considerably easier for them to bring me here.

I don't know how long I was awake when a key card unlocked the door and a man in a military uniform entered. (It was only later I came to think of this man as the General.) Behind him two other men entered and quickly, efficiently handcuffed my wrists and ankles, then left, throwing me to the floor as they did so. The first man then said I should be worried, I was really in trouble. I had ended up where I shouldn't be. On the wrong side of the war. And I would tell them what they wanted to know, everything they wanted to know, or I would be tortured at great length. Then he left the room and I passed out again.

When I come to, it's because something wakes me. Five young men are being shoved into my room. My wrists and ankles feel like they're on fire. The cuffs cut into them like dull knives. I wonder if I've ever been in so much pain, then think perhaps I'll soon be in considerably more when I'm tortured. That's the first thing I remember, they said they were going to torture me. The five men, who I understand to be my five new cellmates, have their arms and legs free. They sit around me, their backs pressed against the wall, like a family sitting around a Christmas turkey, if the turkey lay on the bare floor in front of them. They talk to each other, not much but a little, and do their best to ignore me. There is barely room for all six of us in the cell, they're almost on top of me, and yet it seems strangely normal that they don't acknowledge my existence. If I were in their place I might do the same. I understand that they are young soldiers being court-martialled. Their crime is refusing to get in the planes and fly their assigned missions. Hundreds and hundreds of soldiers are refusing to fly their missions, not because they've become pacifists or because they're against these wars, but because they're afraid their planes will explode. Being shot down by enemy fire means being a brave soldier, and what's more, it almost never happens, but being in a plane that explodes for no discernible reason seems stupid and makes them feel almost supernaturally afraid. That's why they've been crammed into this cell with me. All the other cells are full. Overfull. Overpacked. Because so many soldiers are now refusing to explode in the sky for no reason.

In general, I don't read books that feature torture. My nervous system simply isn't strong enough. The fact that torture is happening, that it is likely that someone somewhere is being tortured right now, as we speak, often feels to me like one of the main reasons I don't want to live in this world. I don't want to read about torture and I certainly don't want to write about it, but what happened ridiculously, sadistically happened (and also didn't happen), and if I'm going to tell my story, there is really no way I can avoid the topic.

If humanity is ever put on trial—and I have no concept who or what might make such a thing possible—the fact that we commit genocide should be enough to condemn us. But the fact that we torture would condemn us in some condemnation of infinite overload. I can think of no more convincing evidence that we represent a universe gone wrong. A species that tortures is a kind of evil, a kind of animal, I will never understand. There are plenty of other books that give the details, I will not give any of them here. The fact that we torture would be enough to condemn us. But, as most of us know, condemnation and judicial punishment depend not on the crime committed but on the values and world view of the authority that sits in judgment. When I think of why I might want to die, so many of my reasons are weak and self-pitying, but one reason I always find convincing is that I don't want to live in a world where people imprison and torture others. I don't want to live in a world that contains torture. But we don't get to decide which world we live in. We only get to decide whether or not we try to do anything about it.

I remember, a long time ago, reading a definition of sanity. Sanity is knowing that to be a full person one must behave differently in different situations. That one behaves one way in bed with a lover and a different way when being interrogated by the Gestapo. That with a lover one was honest, truthful, one opened one's heart. But with the Gestapo one said nothing or skilfully lied. Lying there on the floor of the cell, I thought I had devised a strategy to get through the torture and interrogation. I do not think this strategy would work in reality. This book is not reality. I knew I wouldn't be able to stay silent so I would talk and talk and lie and lie. For everything I said that was perhaps factually true, I would make sure I said at least ten things that were factually untrue, and do my best to make the untrue things sound considerably more plausible than the true ones. (Once again, I don't think this strategy would work in reality, but as literature, I told myself, we can see what it does.) And that is what I planned to do. How I had planned to write about it here. But when the time came, I did no such thing.

They take me to another room, they drag me along many hallways to get there, as they drag me I let my body go limp, and once there they ask me a long series of questions. This first time they don't torture me and I find myself thinking that in the long run it might not be so bad. There are hundreds of questions and I answer the ones that sound most harmless. I no longer remember what any of these questions were. They tell me I already know what they want to know. I think: I don't already know what you want to know. They want to know exactly how the people on the thin strip of land are making the planes explode. The people on the thin strip of land aren't making the planes explode. This is not the answer they want to hear. Then they bring me back to this cell with the five young soldiers who, for some not hard to imagine reason, each don't want to get into a mysteriously exploding plane. I have been interrogated, my hands remain cuffed behind my back, I can no longer feel my arms. I don't know what I feel, if I feel anything. I can't remember any of the questions they just asked me, or what I answered, though I know they asked me many questions and I said many things in response. I have a strange feeling, almost like a sickness, that I am getting what I deserve, because of my stupid plan to come here, my non-plan to see what lay on the other side of my fragmented imagination of war.

I lie on the floor of the cell, passing in and out of consciousness, unable to feel my arms, my shoulders and neck burning as if on fire. When momentarily awake, I listen to the short, banal conversations of my cellmates, who continue to ignore me. They are talking about sports. I'm not ever sure which sports. All the sports. The players who are better than others. They do not acknowledge my existence nor include me in their conversations, which is good because I know absolutely nothing about sports. I have hallucinations that I'm actually not here, that they don't see me because I'm not here and therefore they aren't really ignoring me. I also have hallucinations that they are the ones who are not here, that they're figments of my imagination. Both these explanations seem more plausible than the simple fact that we can all be stuck in this very small room together for so long with all of them, never once, even for a moment, acknowledging my existence. But in my moments of lucidity, I also realize the least plausible explanation is also the most factually true. (And it's also true that I didn't acknowledge or speak to any of them.) My five cellmates are allowed out of the room three times a day for meals and once every other day for exercise. Each time the door is opened, each one of them carefully steps over me as they are led out of the room. I don't know if the fact that they don't kick me or step on me on their way out should be seen as a small mercy or as yet another way they continue to ignore me, to in no way acknowledge my existence. I am not fed nor am I allowed any exercise. If I think I'm hallucinating, lack of food, lack of sunlight, and lack of proper sleep might all be predominant reasons. But I'm also in so much pain. I begin to think of hallucinating as a respite from feeling only physical pain. One by one, the others step over me as they're marched back into the small cell. Their conversations, though I must have logged hours upon hours of them, rarely stay with me. Food, sports, sex, violence, movies, television. Even though there is nothing else for me to listen to, nothing else to distract me, I suppose I'm still not really listening.

Over the coming weeks, many people are involved in interrogating and torturing me, too many to name, and I have difficulty keeping track of them all. I have trouble understanding what I'm saying in response to each question, following the action, following my growing feelings of absolute powerlessness. I had no idea it was possible to feel so powerless. However, the one I am able to keep track of is the General. I suppose his job is to play the good cop because regularly he says he wants to be my friend. If he really wanted to be my friend he wouldn't be torturing me or stand calmly in the corner of the room as I'm being tortured. I can't remember why I started calling him the General, but in my mind the name sticks. But why am I calling him the General? It gives him power over me. Instead I will start calling him the Popsicle, which makes him into a joke, which is all he really is. Even though here he is a joke with the power to cause me unbearable levels of pain. From the very beginning I knew this trip was a mistake, and while I am being tortured I know it even more intensely. After a certain period of time, it might have been a week or might have been a month, the Popsicle takes me out for a walk. It is the first time I've been outside since my arrival. He says he wants to demonstrate that he's my friend by taking me outside, taking me out into the fresh air, into the sunlight that at first almost blinds me. He wants us to talk.

—You're not being very helpful. We really thought you'd be more co-operative.

—That's funny. I was hoping I'd be considerably less co-operative.

—You know I'm here to help you.

—You're not.

—Is it because you're an artist you're so stubborn? You should really consider being more helpful.

—I know.

I can feel, by the way he pauses, that's not what he was expecting me to say. A long, tentative pause as we continue to slowly walk. We are walking so slowly because my legs will barely carry me. Every step contains a world of its own frailty. But we are walking. He is matching his pace to my own. We are walking so slowly it seems we are barely moving at all. He continues:

—It's just we think the soldiers you fought alongside know something. We want to know what they know. And we think you can tell us.

—They don't know anything.

—It's noble of you to protect them. But you're only going to do yourself harm in the end.

—I'm not protecting them. They don't know any more about it than you do.

—We think they're practising witchcraft.

—They're not. They're soldiers just like you are. Only they're good at it.

Almost before I've finished speaking, swiftly and without warning, the Popsicle punches me hard in the gut and I fall to the ground like it was nothing. Like a sheet of paper folded in two. Day by day I am slowly learning how weak I have become. I am actually too weak to get back up. After several tries he manages to pull me to my feet and we continue our stroll.

—Do you want to go back in the room? Do you want the torture to continue? Because I'll level with you, there's nothing we'd like more. We're here, out for a nice stroll together, having a nice chat, and you need to go ruin it by insulting me to my face.

—Either way, you're sending me to the room. I'm not planning to get through this alive.

Perhaps I sound brave but I'm not. I am so afraid I barely even know who I am or what I'm saying. ("They're soldiers just like you are. Only they're good at it.") I barely even register that this Popsicle is seriously considering the possibility of witchcraft, that witchcraft was the only insane explanation he has left.

—You're not planning to get out of here alive?

—No.

—I mean, what the hell kind of attitude is that?

—I'm a writer.

He looks at me. He's a Popsicle and I'm a writer. (But he's obviously not a Popsicle, not even a General, and perhaps I'm not even a writer.) I wonder what he knows about writers. As if reading my mind, he says:

—You probably think I don't know anything about literature, about writers. But I read. I've read Kafka, Bernhard, Musil. I mention the Europeans because I imagine you're the kind of writer who likes that sort of thing. I've also read *War and Peace*. Have you?

I admit that I haven't.

—I didn't think so. But you probably have read *The Brothers Karamazov*.

I admit that he's right. That I haven't read Tolstoy but I have read Dostoyevsky. I feel I'm admitting far more than I wish.

—I read literature because I believe it reveals a great deal about human psychology, about why men do what they do. I won't lie to you. Most of my colleagues in the armed forces don't read literature, though I like to believe there was a time when they did. Back in the good old days. But then again, maybe not. I also won't lie to you about something else. I'm trying to break you. I want to break you so you'll tell us what we want to know. Telling you that I read literature is all part of this, a part of the psychological warfare we hope will eventually make you break. Taking you out for this walk. Everything is part of it. Do you understand?

I say that I do.

—You might think what we're doing to you is sadistic. But we're giving you the light treatment, the kind we use to get actually factual information. Things you know that might be of use to us. To get you to say whatever we want you to say, for that we do worse. We have other places we'd send you. Tell me you're going to co-operate with us. Don't make me send you there. You don't want to see our worst.

He then threatened to kidnap my wife and children, bring them here so I could hear their screams. But, of course, I didn't have a wife or children (I actually can't stand children), and what was strange is I think the Popsicle already knew this. He saw the way I was looking at him, I suppose as if he was senile or something, and stopped talking, thinking over what he had moments ago said, catching himself in the process:

—That's right. You don't have a family. I was just giving you the normal threats. You do this often enough and you end up on autopilot.

But what was even stranger is I started to think that he made this slip on purpose, to make himself seem more human, that he too could make mistakes, so I would begin to trust him and therefore eventually confide in him.

I had a plan to tell them everything but the truth, to make up story after surreal, fantastical story, but I didn't manage to follow this plan. I don't know what I said. I said anything that came to me alongside the pain. In pain I think I must have screamed: They can blow up the planes with their minds. I think I must have screamed this many times. Over and over again. With their minds. But they can't blow up the planes with their minds. Who can do that and why would anyone believe me? What kind of book do I think I'm writing? Or living? When the pain hits, you just say fucking anything. I knew that already, but now I know it more. I have wanted to die for so long and now, finally, I have a good, immediate reason to do so. With this reason, I ask myself, do I want to die more or less than before? Strangely, I think the answer might be less. How could that possibly be true? (Perhaps reminiscent of the Karl Marx quip: "There is only one antidote to mental suffering, and that is physical pain.")

This book is not reality. But why is it not reality? This book is not reality because it is an adventure story, and I am the hero, and therefore no matter what happens to me, no matter how horrible or savage, I will survive it, or at least that's what I think right now when I also think I'm becoming delirious and when I also think I'm losing my mind. My survival is a power fantasy, a fantasy of power. A hallucination. I'm leaving out so many details that happened and didn't happen, this chapter shorter than all others since I'd prefer to relive it as briefly as possible.

When I'm tossed back into my cell, bruised and broken, barely alive, my five cellmates are right where I left them, sitting lined up on the floor, backs pressed smoothly against the wall. I expect them to continue ignoring me, much as they had before, but the moment they're certain the guards are out of earshot, the tallest of them leans forward and speaks:

—Can I ask you something?

For a moment I consider my options. Should I continue ignoring them in the same way that they had up until this moment ignored me? Instead I attempt to make my reply as cold and unforgiving as possible under the circumstances. In retrospect, I realize that if I had been in better shape, I might have reacted in a considerably more forgiving manner.

Me: We were in this cell together for weeks and weeks, and none of you ever spoke to me or bothered to acknowledge my existence.

The tallest of them: I know. But now we want to ask you something.

One at a time, they each tell me their names, but I don't bother to mentally note them, so I will now simply give them the condescending, generic names that in my heart of hearts I truly believe they deserve.

Moe (the tallest of them): We want to ask you something because there is something we don't understand. There's no one else here. You're the only one who can help.

Larry: We had all gotten out of here. Maybe you didn't notice, but they let us out. We were free. We had all agreed to get in our planes and fly our assigned missions. They have so few qualified pilots now that they agreed to let bygones be bygones. Court martial over and we could simply get back in our planes and go back to work.

Howard: But then him, he was about to get into his plane when he started screaming. He just stood there on the tarmac screaming and screaming. He couldn't stop.

Tom: It's true. That's what happened. That's what I did.

Moe: Which is strange enough. But then I started screaming as well. Like the screaming was contagious and leapt from his body into mine. And I couldn't stop either.

Larry: And then I started screaming.

Jerry: You can see where this is headed. A few moments later, it had happened to all of us. All five of us were standing there on the tarmac, in front of our respective planes, screaming our lungs out, screaming ourselves hoarse, with our commanding officers shouting at us to stop our screaming, stop our screaming and get into our planes, to fly our respective missions. We could barely hear the shouted orders over the endless din of our collective screams.

Tom: And we all stood there just screaming and screaming until they forcibly pulled us off the runway and threw us back in here.

I had a splitting headache, as if my skull had been cracked in two, as if the five of them had been screaming not out there among the planes but here inside my head.

Me: Why are you telling me this?

Moe: We wanted your professional opinion.

Larry: We thought you, as someone who specializes in political dissent, might know why this happened to us.

Howard: Might know why we all started screaming and couldn't get into our planes.

I of course didn't know. I thought it was quaint they thought of me as someone who specialized in political dissent. I specialized in no such thing. In such situations, honesty is always the best policy.

Me: I actually don't know.

I also don't know exactly when it was I began to think, or rather to recall, that there must be a history of political dissidents who, while under arrest, utilized the prison as a place to organize and radicalize others. In the fact that these soldiers were refusing to get into their planes I sensed an opening. I've always felt that for activism it greatly helps to have such an opening, some brief fissure where the system has momentarily broken down and into which one can move and create movement. If things are no longer as they've always been, perhaps this creates the possibility, or at least the thought, that everything could be even more different. Also, I was here, unlike any place I'd ever been before, a place where there was obviously much work to be done. And something else: when all odds are stacked against me, that is perhaps the moment I most come to life. So it was worth a try. But what, precisely, was the best approach for me to take? Who were these screaming men who didn't even know why they were screaming, and what could I do or say to turn their screams against this war and, more importantly, against the government that had sent them here to fight it? What did they care about, what values, that I could confront them with? Why had they joined the army in the first place? That was a question that struck a nerve with me, or at least a question I genuinely wanted to know the answer to, so I started there.

Me: Maybe to know why you were screaming, you need to start from the beginning.

Moe: Which beginning?

Me: To start before you joined the army.

Larry: The air force.

Me: To start before you joined the air force. To think a little about motives, why did you join, what were your motives?

Howard: What were our motives for joining the air force?

Me: Yes.

Jerry: My father was in the air force so I joined the air force. I think that's about the same for all of us.

Everyone agreed. It seems the air force was a family business. Then the first crack, the first moment of dissent.

Tom: That's not the reason I joined.

Everyone looks at Tom. Tom doesn't say a word, he actually looks terrified, wondering what he's done, why his story is different. Does he really want to be different from the others? We're now all waiting to hear his reason, and it suddenly seems to me that I've never wanted to know anything so badly in my entire life. I want to know the answer so badly that I don't even notice my migraine anymore.

Tom: I don't know why I joined, but my father wasn't in the air force, he was a barber, so that can't be the reason. I must have joined for a scholarship. It was the only way I could imagine being able to afford going to school. Now I can't even remember why I wanted to go to school. Or *if* I wanted to. But if I think back, that's what I originally remember telling myself was the reason.

Could I work with this? Four fathers and a scholarship? I noticed that my concentration on the task at hand— attempting to convince these five sitting on the floor, each leaning back against the wall, to in some way change their political views—had at least partly taken my mind off the physical pain. I noticed the pain a bit less now. This was a side effect of our conversation, but one, for obvious reasons, I desired.

Me: When you joined the air force, what did you imagine it would be like?

Moe: We're not here for therapy.

Me: Maybe to understand why you were screaming, you need a little therapy.

Larry: That makes sense.

Howard: I think I imagined saving the world. Saving the world from the enemy.

Me: Who was the enemy?

Howard: You know the enemy.

Jerry: I definitely didn't imagine saving the world. I think I thought it would be more like a job. A good job I could learn to do well.

Tom: I just wanted the scholarship.

Moe: We know you just wanted the scholarship.

Me: And do you all still want to be in the air force now?

That really shut them up. At least for a moment.

Larry: Why were we screaming? Why did the screaming jump from one body to the next? Why couldn't we get into our planes?

Me: I don't know.

Tom: I think I was screaming because I don't want to die. I'm too young. I don't want to die yet.

Me: Maybe the people you drop bombs on also don't want to die.

Howard: It's better not to think about that.

Me: Obviously you are thinking about it or you wouldn't have been screaming.

Larry: No, that can't be it. That can't be the reason.

Jerry: If that's the reason, we still need a solution.

Just then, or sometime around then, the key card slid into its slot and the door slid open. A guard came in and told them to get up. They all got up. I knew the guard wasn't also talking to me so I did not get up. One at a time they stepped over me as I continued to lie there on the floor. The door slid shut and I was alone, my distractions gone, the pain flooding back into my body.

I worry that I'm writing about all of this with too much humour. Like a comedy in a nightmare. I wasn't laughing at the time but do remember thinking: I must keep my sense of humour. When all this is over, if I've survived and even when I haven't, I must try to retain some humour about it all and about the future.

The next time the key card opens the door, they drag me out of the building and throw me in the back of a van. We drive for a very long time. I've lost all track of time. In the van it is hot and I feel I'm running a fever. Or it's cold and I only think it's hot because I'm running a fever. It seems to me I've been unconscious for a very long time before we arrive at our destination and I'm awakened by a soldier shoving a feeding tube down my throat. I realize they think I'm staging a hunger strike, but it's only that I have no appetite and also don't remember them offering me any food. Is it possible I was offered food, refused it, and don't even remember having done so? The feeding tube feels like a knife cutting into my throat. I am in a new place, surrounded by new people, who have decided that a new approach is required to get me to tell them what they want to know. For a moment it strangely feels like I've been upgraded in status to that of an important prisoner in possession of essential information. The nutrition they've just poured down my throat makes it more difficult for me to fall in and out of consciousness, which I quickly realize I miss. What follows is my being asked to describe, at great length, in great detail, everything I saw, heard, and experienced during my somewhat less than a year of living on the thin strip of land. I don't know if I ever had the will to resist, but now I definitely don't have the will to resist. But what do I tell them? I've already told them so much during previous sessions. They say they want to hear it all again and this time I must be extra careful not to leave out a single detail. No detail is irrelevant. Any detail might prove important. What am I telling them now? I realize while I was on the thin strip of land, many must have thought I was a spy, a mole, a double agent, and now I am proving them right. I'm also told this new building I've been brought to is a hospital, that I've been brought to this hospital because I'm ill, running a high fever, but also that they're hoping the illness, the fever, will make me more willing to talk, and they want to keep me alive long enough to hear everything I have to say, but if I don't talk it costs them nothing to let me die. There is no public relations scandal if I die in the hospital of an illness I contracted while unadvisedly exploring this war-torn country. As I'm listening, I'm trying to take in my surroundings. It does seem more like a hospital than any of the previous rooms I've been interrogated in. People die in hospitals all the time.

My arms and legs are once again strapped to the chair. The straps in the hospital are a bit more comfortable than the ones back at the compound. Everything is a bit more comfortable here. But there are still armed guards at each door and I certainly can't come or go as I please. I go exactly where they tell me and each time am led there at gunpoint. They explain that I'll remain strapped to this chair, kept alive, until I've told them everything they want to know. Most of what I recount is the story I've already told in the previous chapter. But they keep asking for more, for further details. And then I actually do remember something I hadn't remembered until that very moment. They got it all out of me, but I managed not to tell them this one stupid little thing. And if I didn't tell them, I'm certainly not going to tell you now.

The Popsicle takes me on at least one more walk. There might have been a third walk, but I mainly remember two. What I recall most about this second walk is the silence. So much silence. This was a new approach. Now he remained silent, waiting for me to talk. We are walking through the grounds of the hospital. It is a small hospital, and we walk around it many times. As was the case before, it feels good simply to be outside, in the air and sunlight. It seems insane to me how little I've been outside since I was first detained. I actually never knew how important it is to spend time outside until this moment. And yet it sickens me that I associate this good feeling with the Popsicle, since he is the only one here to take me outside, and I know this positive association is the actual point of our walks. Due to the medical treatment I've received, I feel a little bit stronger now than I did during our previous excursion and believe I am even walking at something resembling a normal pace. But still slowly. Slowly in silence. Despite feeling physically a bit better, I am sullen and despondent, and in my despondency I become fascinated by the ongoing silence. How clear it is that the Popsicle expects I will be the one to break it. As we round the hospital yet another time, I think he finally realizes it will have to be him:

—You might think the torture is over.

—I don't.

—We're genuinely pleased with how co-operative you've become.

—I'm not.

—I feel we've gotten to know each other a bit over our time

together. Even though we're on opposite sides, even though we have little in common, you can't help but get to know someone when you've gone through an intense experience with them. Would you agree?

—I'd prefer not to.

—That's a reference to Melville's Bartleby. You might have thought I didn't know that.

—No. You read. Your problem isn't that you don't read.

—You see. It's just as I was trying to explain a moment ago. You're getting to know me.

—I suppose.

I sounded like a sullen teenager. A teenager of few words. I wasn't quite following the situation. It felt like he wanted to know what I thought of him, or that he wanted my approval. But why would my captor want my approval? He was just fucking with me, as always, trying to get inside my head. What exactly is the psychology of all those men who tortured me? How many of them were there? Apart from the Popsicle, I learned so little about them. They had been carefully trained. The torture they applied to my body was not an improvisation, it was torture they had been trained to apply, ordained to commit. It was a procedure that went all the way to the top. Like a bomb being dropped, it was official policy to do so. But there was also—at least it seemed to me—a certain pleasure in it. A pleasure in having power over another. Or even a pleasure in someone else's pain. I wasn't certain about that last part. They were playing by the rules, it was a game with a goal, but also a cat playing with a half-dead mouse, batting it back and forth in its paws. The game would have been very different if I'd had the tools to fight back. I now wanted to say something that would get under the Popsicle's skin but really wasn't sure there was any way I could:

—You might be right.

—About what?

—Maybe I have been getting to know you.

—I'm sure you have.

—You think you know better than me. About everything. That you're smarter and more clever and stronger and more powerful. You think in the strategic chess game of life, you're five moves ahead of me and five moves ahead of everyone. You think you can so gracefully hold your boot against my neck because of your guile and skill and talent. And because of this you'll never understand how much of your success and ability to hurt me comes down to simple dumb luck.

He laughed off my slight and we continued walking in silence. I thought a moment longer about what I had just said. He thought he was smarter than me and I thought I was smarter than him. And yet we both knew, in this particular situation, that he had far more power. Then it was his turn to try to shake me:

—You might have already guessed this, but when I was younger I wanted to be a writer. That's why I'm so well-read.

—And why didn't you?

—I don't know. My life took a different turn. I decided to be an adult instead. Contribute to society more directly. When I joined the military, I was very young, practically still a child, but I do remember thinking: Maybe all this will give me something to write about one day.

—Why are you telling me this?

—I want you to see we're not so different. Because I want you to talk to me. I know you'd prefer not to. But we've already started. And I've always thought that when you start, it's important to see it through until the end.

—What kind of books would you have written?

—I don't know. I never got to find out.

I knew I was being manipulated, but it was working anyway. I questioned if he really wanted to be a writer when he was younger or if this was simply the best lie he could come up with. What could a Popsicle, or a General, possibly have to write about? This thought was followed by further silence. Torture was one strategy, and trying to win me over was another, and this walk was part of the second approach.

—There's one thing that strikes me as strange. We haven't received any inquiries into your whereabouts. And when I do a search, no one seems to have noticed you've gone missing. Don't you have any family, any friends?

—Apparently not.

—You must have at least a few friends wanting to know where you are.

—They probably just think I'm lying in bed too depressed to move.

—And they don't check up on you?

—We're not that close.

—That's sad. You must live a really sad life.

—I don't know. Is your life so full of beautiful friends? Don't answer. I can already see where this is going. You're going to tell me you also don't have friends and look at how alike we are and that's why I should confide in you.

—No, I have lots of friends. A beautiful wife, beautiful children.

As we walked in silence, I realized I couldn't help myself. I was talking to the Popsicle because I literally had no one else to talk to. At home, I might not have had friends, but there was always someone to talk to. What a sick world this is where you talk to the enemy because there's literally no one else, feeling so depressed by this idea that, to cheer myself up, I start imagining him as an actual popsicle. A big purple dripping popsicle walking alongside me, two wooden popsicle sticks for legs, angling his frame from side to side with every awkward step. A big purple popsicle with a beautiful popsicle wife and two beautiful popsicle children. Then I imagine him melting, that eventually he will melt away to nothing, leaving a long purple sticky trail behind him, like a purple popsicle snail. And it occurs to me this might be what I most want, for the problems of the world to simply melt away. But the problems of the world will not melt away, we must find tools and strategies to push against them, and I wonder, even here, in this hopeless predicament, what such tools and strategies might be, as the imaginary purple popsicle continues to melt into nothingness beside me.

The day I was moved from my hospital bed back to the prison cell felt like one of the worst days of my life. The same military van drove me back along the same route. In the hospital I was repeatedly interrogated but, apart from the feeding tube, never tortured. I'm not sure why. Maybe my screams would have bothered the other patients. There was better soundproofing back at the compound. Or maybe I was already telling them everything they wanted to know and therefore there was no longer any need to torture me. I was only tortured one more time, the most mild version of the agony they put me through, and apart from that I could feel my life drifting into a dull, empty routine. I had somehow managed to convince them that I don't know why the planes are exploding, so they don't ask me about that anymore. In fact, they now basically seem to think of me as a pretentious idiot who knows nothing, who contains no further useful information.

I was now fed with the other prisoners three times a day, allowed to exercise three times a week, and I was even allowed a few rather mediocre things to read. This was my reward for having been so co-operative, and therefore everything tasted like poison. All moments not spent eating or exercising were spent in solitary confinement. I felt there was so little contact with others so I would not try to spread my ideas. I started to plot how I might best use the few scarce moments granted to me for interaction. Back in my cell, or perhaps another, similar-looking cell, always alone, I began to miss my five screaming friends, wondering if, given enough time, I could have genuinely turned them against the war. The solitary confinement I was now placed in had no room for others, so much smaller than my previous cells, just a little bit larger than coffins, just large (or small) enough for me to stretch out as if I was already dead. Many hours would be spent obsessing over the fact that I might spend the rest of my natural life confined to these conditions. My legal status was dubious, as was the legal status of most of the other prisoners here. I was not under arrest and, as far as I knew, there was no due process I could appeal to.

It was amazing how slowly the time began to crawl, how uneventful each day became, how little I knew about anything happening in the outside world. It was tedious boredom as a way of life, while at the same time I lived in constant irrational fear that at any moment the torture would resume. There was some conversation during mealtimes, but it was carefully monitored—the guards walked through the aisles perpetually eavesdropping—so we tried not to say too much, nothing that would get us in trouble. Most of the time trouble wasn't worth it. And the seating arrangements were rotated each day, meaning I rarely sat with the same person twice, and basically never got to know anyone. I was casually told that at each table, or every other table, or every third table, one of the prisoners eating with us was a spy or snitch or double agent. I never found out if this was true or only a rumour spread to make us more careful about what we said. Where was the opportunity to educate and spread dissent? I tried repeatedly speaking through the walls of my solitary confinement, but there was no one on the other side, or they couldn't hear me, or they simply chose to ignore me. Maybe they ignored me out of a suspicion I was a double agent.

And then something implausible happened. Though, I suppose, no more implausible than anything else I have recounted. One of the soldiers had taken a photograph of me being tortured and apparently sent it to a friend, who later posted it online. (If you are reading this several hundred years from now, and don't know what the Internet is, I suggest you look it up. It was a fascinating time.) I have always thought of myself as a writer who does not have many readers, but one person who had read one of my books saw this photo of me being tortured, recognized me—though at first they weren't sure it was actually me—and spread the word. It wasn't long before every single person who had read my books, and even many who had only heard of them, knew I was being detained on a military base and that I was being tortured. Of course, no one knew exactly why. There was much speculation. One of these readers apparently had an uncle who was a high-ranking official in the military. He began pestering his uncle relentlessly and convinced other family members to do the same. The uncle, mainly to make the pestering stop, decided to investigate the situation, came to the conclusion there was no legal basis for my continued detainment, and gave orders for my release. (With my current level of success as an author, I'm really not sure this could happen in reality. But I dare you to tell me this couldn't happen. This book isn't reality. It's fiction. With all the ethical problems that writing fiction entails.) And, more importantly, I do not believe this was the main reason for my release. They were sick of me. They had decided I didn't know anything. They were surprised at the reaction to the leaked photo, unable to accurately ascertain the extent of my celebrity, and therefore unable to ascertain the degree of the public relations fiasco that would result from my continued incarceration or accidental death. I was not yet much of a martyr, and by quietly releasing me they reduced the possibility I might ever become one. Saved by the *deus ex machina* of the Internet. Just as quickly as it started, it was over. Bye-bye, nice knowing (and torturing) you, as if there was no responsibility and nothing had happened.

The moment they hand me back my knapsack I look inside it. I don't understand exactly what I expect to see. Perhaps all the objects inside it smashed up and destroyed, all the objects looking the way I feel. But as soon as I look I also realize what I most want to see again: the cassettes, the interviews, my only record of my time on that thin strip of land. I don't know why I'm so surprised, but all the cassettes are still intact. Did they listen to them? If they listened, why didn't they erase them? Why did they simply hand them back to me? If they didn't listen, what could the reason possibly be? Lack of curiosity? Some bureaucratic entanglement in which the left hand didn't know that the right hand wanted them to carefully go through the contents of my bag and glean the information most required? It occurred to me that perhaps they didn't have a cassette player and couldn't be bothered to track one down. Perhaps the archaic nature of the technology was all that saved the cassettes from further surveyance.

The Popsicle came to see me off. Right away, before I had said a word, he looked me in the eye and began:

—If you write about this, write about me. Make me an interesting character. But if you use my real name, I'll sue you for everything you're worth. And I'll win too. You can be sure of that.

This didn't occur to me previously, while I was writing it all down, but I fear now that I have made him an interesting character, given him his wish, though hopefully I've also made him a popsicle-flavoured joke. Either way, I didn't use his real name. But I'm not going to go back and rewrite it now. Somehow those bastards always get their way and there's no point in pretending they don't. Which doesn't mean I wouldn't kill him in a second if I ever had the chance. Not that it would do any good. There are a million more where he came from. It probably wouldn't even make me feel any better. Which I suppose is also the reason I don't, right now, fictionally kill him in print. In my mind, I spit in his eye and the next time he gets into a plane it spontaneously explodes. He was the good cop who made the entire evil business run more smoothly. Because we both knew, especially in war, especially when you're the warmongering aggressor, there are no good cops, only bad faith and bad actors.

As I was awaiting the flight that would take me home, I looked up. In the distance I saw a formation of warplanes, most likely on their way to drop bombs. One of the planes in the formation exploded. I smiled. It was probably the first time I had smiled in a very long time. But, at the same time, I feared or I knew it was the smile of someone who had already died.

4: Some Future

When I got to pretty much this point in writing a first draft,
I did something that absolutely terrified me. I sent it back
to the thin strip of land and asked what they thought. I sent
them the manuscript, or at least the first three-quarters
of it. I didn't feel comfortable writing about them, even
as fiction, if this book is to be considered fiction, without
their commentary or consent. I had a contact who claimed
they could smuggle it back in for me. I gave this person
three spiral-bound photocopies of the first three chapters
and asked if they could find Goldman, Zana, and Huerta,
give them one copy each. I didn't know if Goldman, Zana,
and Huerta were even all still alive, but I hoped they were.
I didn't know if it was even fair to ask them to read what
I had written. On the title page of each photocopy was a
handwritten note thanking them for their hospitality and
explaining that if they wanted to share my draft-so-far with
anyone or everyone, they were welcome to do so and I was
open to all comments and suggestions.

I then waited over a year and thought I would probably
never hear anything about it again. Eventually I forgot I
had even sent the photocopies. It seemed to me almost
like something I had done not in reality but in a dream. But
then I got a package. In the package were four letters. (Not
three as I had expected.) Letters that I now cherish basically
more than anything else I own. I knew I had to read them,
but I couldn't quite bring myself to do so. I was too afraid.
I left the letters on my desk. Every day I would stare at the

envelope for a while before attempting to write. And then, every few weeks, I would muster the courage, pull one of the letters out from the envelope, and begin.

The letter from Goldman

It was fascinating to read your manuscript. No one, to the best of my knowledge, has ever written about me before. Perhaps the military, the enemy, has a dossier on me, but I'm sure the writing is not nearly as good.

But to begin with the negative, there is definitely one section I take issue with. The scene when I so smoothly and effortlessly turn to shoot the assassin out of the tree. We both know that didn't happen. I'm disappointed in you. I don't see why you need to embellish. I don't see why you need to add such sensationalistic details. It cheapens your account, fictionalized or otherwise. Isn't what we're doing, what we're building, impressive enough, without having to make me some superhuman assassin with eyes in the back of my head?

What's so strange is, when I wrote it, I didn't think I was embellishing anything. I really believed I was remembering it exactly as it happened. All the details, every moment. In fact—and I don't quite know how to explain this—I still remember it happening. But I don't know what to think, it must have been a memory I made up. (I don't exactly understand how.) And then I think back to a passage I'd written earlier: "Why was I willing to write about violence but not about sex? Because that's the culture I was raised in, having been taught sex was nasty but violence was okay." That perfect shot I remembered her making, turning her body effortlessly to make it, the assassin falling from the

148

distant tree, was some sort of symbol of this upbringing, the ways it has lodged into my imagination, influencing not only my writing but, it seems, my memory itself. Her letter continued:

Apart from that one rather ridiculous lapse in judgment, your telling felt fairly accurate, or at least accurate from the distance of your outsider perspective. It was especially strange for me to read about your torture and interrogation. So many of us have been through it, often so much worse than you experienced. It might be hard for you to understand the degree to which, because you are a foreigner, they really went easy on you. I mean, you are a foreigner from my perspective, but from their perspective you're basically one of them. You grew up on the same streets, have the same cultural references. The fact that they threatened to let you die, but did not actually let you die, is also a clear sign of the preferential treatment you received. When they take a crack at us, they do so as if we were unknowable beasts that can withstand any and all mistreatment. Even the fact that they eventually released you grants you a degree of nervous respect I am sure I would not have been given. Under similar conditions I would have most likely died in there sooner or later. Many we know will never be released. We didn't tell you about that part of our struggle. We focus on what can be done. Count yourself lucky.

There is another thing I should mention. Even though you told them everything, we were careful to tell you nothing, to tell you as little as possible, to hide from you anything and everything that might be of eventual use to our many enemies. It wasn't that we didn't trust you. I mean, we didn't trust you, but that was not the most

149

important reason for our behaviour. What you don't know about, you can't write about (also can't reveal under the pressure of torture or coercion). We didn't want you to have to make the hard choices in the writing of your book. We collectively decided it would be far better for us to make those decisions for you, and future events bore out the wisdom of our decision. So don't be too upset with yourself for breaking under pressure. I suspect only minimal harm was done.

If I think hard now about what I want to say to you—if I interrogate myself, so to speak—I realize I do have a kind of wish. A wish for you and a wish for your eventual book. Because there is so much your book leaves out about our emancipatory project. I know it cannot include everything, but is it really necessary to leave out so much? What about children who had never gone to school, whose parents had never been to school either, now having a chance to receive an education? How proud they are, how proud their families feel, that they can be the first generation able to do so? And an education where they learn not just what some teachers forcefeed them, but where each student has a say as to how and what they learn. What about women whose mothers and grandmothers were only allowed to cook, clean, and raise children, and who are now part of a generation that is active in every role and at every level of society? You weren't here, you didn't see our past, our history, so perhaps it's difficult for you to understand how far we've come and how quickly. And you never mentioned how amazing the food is, you never appreciated how with so little we are able to prepare meal after meal that's so delicious. When you were here, could you feel how real we are with each other? How we tell each other the truth and hold each other accountable? You need to do that when your lives are in each other's hands, you need to trust completely. But I believe we do so not just when we're fighting but in all areas of our life together. In fact, I know we do.

By the way, when we sent you up over the wall, we were definitely not sending you toward a certain death. We assumed you would be easily and painlessly captured, they would come to realize who you were, and after a tedious and bureaucratic process they would eventually send you back from whence you came. It was obviously worse than we thought, everything seems to be worse than one can foresee or imagine these days, but in the end that is basically what happened. If they had captured us all, as I have already mentioned, our fate would have been immeasurably worse.

What else is there to say? Things here continue in their ongoing mess of beauty and fear. I won't go into all the details, but it often seems to me a great miracle I'm still alive. Alive and happy to say that morale here remains remarkably high. Almost everyone I talk to realizes what we have is important, and that gives us all the daily strength to put in the work, to continue fighting in order to ensure it all functions. If we fail, one thing I know for certain is that it will not have been because of a lack of commitment or a lack of effort. Like everyone in the world, we don't know what will happen next. But for now, we continue to survive.

Then she signed her name. And upon seeing the name— not Goldman but her actual name—I suddenly realized something insane. I can't believe I didn't realize this before.

When I was being interrogated, when I told the story from beginning to end, each and every time, I only ever used the names Zana, Huerta, and Goldman. I never used actual names—which, strangely, I now also have to admit, I'm no longer sure I even correctly remember. (Seeing her name at the bottom of the letter, I realize I'd had it slightly wrong the entire time.) Zana, Huerta, and Goldman were the names I used in my little notebook, and those were the names I continued to use each and every time. They must have asked me for real, more accurate names, but I always repeated that the names I was using were the only names they ever told me, the only names I knew. So, though under interrogation I sold them out (to the best of my ability, since I apparently didn't have enough information to truly do so), it was not quite as bad as I'd previously thought. I didn't give names. Or I did give names but always the names I'd made up.

I remember watching the movie *Purple Rain* when I was a teenager. Or, actually, all I remember, correctly or incorrectly, is that for the entire movie the character played by Prince, in his personal life, was a fuck-up and an asshole. (Artistically he was, of course, consistently brilliant.) Then at the end of the movie he pulls himself together and decides to become a decent person. At the time I thought that someday my life would be like that. No matter how much I fucked it up, sooner or later, in time for the end of the movie, I would pull myself together and set everything right. During my trip, all such thoughts left my mind—I only wondered if I might live or die, and then how to make the most of my time with those on the thin strip of land— but now that I've returned home once again, I can't help but consider what it means to live here and how I might do a better job. So many times I've heard that the personal is political, but I worry my life doesn't clearly enough reflect this fact. Since I'm not doing enough. But then again, perhaps most of us aren't. If we were, the world would be in considerably better shape.

I also so clearly remember that year that Prince, David Bowie, and Leonard Cohen died. All in the same year. (There was also an election that year, an election we no longer talk about.) Prince, Bowie, and Cohen are three such different artists, but they are all figures—perhaps mainly because they work in the very specific art form of popular music—whose art touched so many people in so many different ways, whose words became so fully integrated into so many different people's daily lives. Their work really connects. Would anything I ever wrote have even a fraction of that kind of importance in anyone's life? Or, even if it did, how many people? A few dozen? A few hundred? A few thousand? At any rate, not nearly enough to even begin to change the world.

I am listening back to the tapes. So many interviews. Each person being interviewed speaking so clearly and carefully. Realizing, as they were saying it, that what they were explaining to me was precious and important. I transcribe a few lines and then stop transcribing, just listen.

—What's so hard to describe is the very specific feeling of living here.

—Do you think it's important to describe it? Is it necessary?

—I don't know. You're here interviewing me, so that makes me want to. I want to put something onto the tape, put my voice on the tape saying something necessary, that gets to the heart of the matter.

—So then what does it feel like to live here?

I cringe at the sound of my own voice, the sound of myself
trying so hard to be a good little interviewer, to ask the right
questions, to get everything I can out of them.

—It's this feeling that you can't assume anything, you can
never be on autopilot, every thought you have, as you have
it, you also have to pause and ask yourself: Am I just doing
things the old way, as I've always done them, or am I instead
fully doing them in the spirit of our new experiment? And it
can't be about beating yourself up if you're doing it wrong.
It has to be about the possibility of this new situation, in
finding joy in this new sense of possibility. Because if we
survive, it's not we who will fully experience these new possibilities. It's our children and their children.

—But still you have to do your best to live it now.

—Yes, you have to live it now. There's no other way. You
can't wait for the future. You have to make the future
through your attempts to live it now.

I'm trying to remember the face of the woman speaking.
I only interviewed her once, only met her once, and in my
faulty memory her face blurs into all the others. My time on
the thin strip of land was such an experience, maybe the only
true experience I've had in my life, and yet I find it difficult
to accurately remember it. So many of the moments small
and large, so many of the people and faces, all blur together
in my recollections of them. I don't know if I'm writing what
actually happened or to what degree I'm reinventing it all,
making it more the way I wanted it to be. I often think that

memory is like a premonition. Remembering something in the past is a bit like feeling it might someday happen in the future.

—You started by saying it's hard to describe the specific feeling of living here.

—Yes.

—So what is that feeling? Why did you choose to describe it that way?

—I don't know. It's a feeling of uncertainty. Of being on unsteady ground. But it's also a feeling of *wanting* to be on unsteady ground. It doesn't always feel good. But, for me at least, it always feels necessary. They say Jesus walked on water—don't get me wrong, I'm not religious, I'm just searching for a good analogy—because for me living here is not like walking on water but like walking on quicksand, walking on quicksand but most of the time still managing, step after step, to glide along the surface of it. You know that it's quicksand, that with every step there's the possibility you might begin to sink, so there is a kind of joy and relief that with every step you remain upright, that you don't begin to sink down.

I stop listening, rewind the tape, go back and listen to it again from the beginning in order to continue transcribing. I have to listen to each interview so many times to get it all down, have a full transcription before I can begin editing, endless afternoons spent listening and transcribing, in the process reliving it all, living in the past and the present at the same time.

The letter from Huerta

I read your manuscript. We all did. Occasionally at night, when there's nothing left to talk about, we find ourselves talking about it, especially the section that takes place here. It's strange to talk about yourself seen through the lens of someone else, and what's more someone who has lived such different experiences. It's strange to talk about yourself after someone far away has turned some aspects—but only *some* aspects—of your life into fiction. That said, it's often quite fun to talk about your manuscript among ourselves. We're definitely not polite about it. By spending so much time with you here, while at the same time knowing you're a writer, I suppose we have already implicitly given you permission to write about us. Maybe others did so more explicitly, I'm not sure. At any rate, I don't believe there's any stopping you now, so I might as well give you my blessing.

I do like the name you have chosen for me. I believe my namesake must be Dolores Huerta. I'm afraid to admit I actually know rather little about her. She was an activist, fighting for workers' rights, and fought tirelessly her entire life in a context that is so different from our own. And perhaps Cesar Chavez got more credit than she did, or at least he used to, which is rather unfair. Why are things like this when it comes to the reputations of men versus women? But of course I already know why. I feel so proud of how much equality we've managed to create here in such a short time. Clearly there is still such a long way to go, but I was originally not convinced we would even make it this far. So now I don't want to repeat my previous mistake by doubting we will be able to take all of this further. And if I don't live to see it, maybe my children will. Or maybe their children. The important thing is to continue believing that it might be possible. Or, at least, that's what I keep telling myself. But we have already come so far.

Now on to a few criticisms, at least one or two. It occurs to me that you have done a rather poor job of describing how our assemblies work. (Or our "meetings," as you call them.) Our assemblies are the very centre of our lived political practice and that means it is so important to describe them correctly and evocatively. I understand that if you do not really live here—mostly meaning if you are unable to understand and speak the language and therefore unable to fully participate in the assemblies—it is difficult to get a true feel for all their twists and turns, for all their intricacies. And I'm not sure if what's important is for you to convey all the rules and regulations that govern the assemblies, or the other set of guidelines that allow the various levels and communities to interconnect. But what I hope to make clear to you are the ways in which, if one chooses to fully participate—and I know not everyone does—you really feel you have a voice, and that voice over time can concretely shape the society in which you live. I'm not exactly sure how to explain the feeling, but it is as if, over the years, and sometimes even more quickly, you can actually see it happening.

I want to try to give at least one concrete example. When we first started, when we first took over, there were so many questions that we almost didn't know where to begin. How to organize all the challenges we faced and how not to get lost in the enormity of it all. We divided ourselves into committees and each committee was responsible for making proposals and recommendations for how to proceed on their particular topic: energy, goods, water, justice, defence—there were so many I almost can't remember them all. These committees were also divided by region, and at regular intervals all the committees on a specific topic would come together for an interregional assembly to discuss their findings. I myself was not on any of the energy committees, but nonetheless I found myself at the first interregional energy gathering. I was there as a representative for the business and economic department, to report back at my own assembly as to the economic feasibility of the various proposals on offer. In this capacity, I would ask many questions during the meetings, and unfortunately too many of my questions had to do with what things cost—not always in terms of money but in terms of other resources, or in some harder to define, but also important, general sense—a topic I actually found quite boring but for obvious reasons necessary.

At this assembly there was a teenager I had never seen before. I unthinkingly assumed he was the son of one of the other representatives, and for that reason paid no attention to him. But when his turn came to speak, everyone listened, no one discounted him because of his youth, or assumed because they were older they naturally knew better. I believe this is the kind of openness many of us were feeling at that time. He was so nervous speaking in front of us, you could hear his voice shake with every word, but he was also prepared. He knew what he wanted to say. He told us he had figured out how to build a fairly simple but effective vertical-axis windmill and that he could teach us. It was a closet-sized, easily used device that anyone could build and would provide a certain amount of energy for daily use. He then brought out a maquette from his bag. He took out a folding hand fan, spread it open with a flick of his wrist, and proceeded to fan the maquette to make it spin. As it did so, it lit up a small light bulb. It was basically a comical—even pathetic—demonstration, and some of us even laughed a little when the light bulb lit up. But that didn't mean we weren't listening and weren't giving him the full benefit of the doubt. Right now I'm writing to you by hand under an overhead light bulb that's powered by just such a vertical-axis windmill that is slowly turning in the breeze out in the yard, a few feet from my back door. Many of us have them now. I did not build this one myself, but many of us did. If we had more material, perhaps everyone could have them. When it's windy it really does the job. They can easily be built from scrap, so as we continue to scavenge our surroundings, more and more waist-high windmills can be built all the time. And that teenager now knows that one shaky presentation given at a single interregional assembly can be adopted and ripple outward for years to come. And other young people have now heard this story and therefore know that if they have an idea, they should definitely not keep it to themselves. They know what the committees and assemblies are for—to share their ideas and be heard. For me, this is the true spirit of our endeavour, and the assemblies are one of the main places it can happen. I'm not sure if this is the best example, because it happened almost like magic, or more specifically like science, but it is a clear example that finds its echo in so many other, different kinds of examples that impact every level of our society.

I also question, or ask you to further reflect upon, your

understanding of, and relationship to, violence. From my perspective you seem overly fascinated by the fact that we are so many women with guns, and you are perhaps not fascinated enough by all the other things we have accomplished or are working toward. Violence is seductive, and therefore I urge you not to be seduced. I am not a violent person by nature. I don't know if I believe in violence, but I definitely don't care for it. However, if I see a man who is about to rape—or has just raped—one of the women I live and work alongside, or for that matter any woman, I can aim my rifle and kill that man with absolutely vengeful efficiency. I have now been trained to do so and feel no remorse. Too many women have been killed. Too many women have been raped. Rape is a weapon of war, meant to brutalize and humiliate us, and here, as you well know, we are surrounded by war on all sides. If I kill a man who rapes, it is no great loss. If he doesn't want to be killed, the change he has to make is simple enough. I hope by explaining this I am not in any way further sensationalizing our violence. I simply wish to convey what is at stake, the absolute intensity for us of what is at stake. If you fight us with respect, if you treat us with respect, we will return the same respect back to you. When I think of the future, maybe if we can't eliminate war, we can at least start to change the way it is fought. I don't yet know with what methods such changes are most likely to occur. These are the kinds of questions I ask myself almost every day now.

In fact, time and time again, I find myself so deeply questioning our endeavour, working to ask myself the really hard questions, hoping that in the struggle I never think I have it all figured out, never let myself off the hook.

I don't know if this is actually necessary or only a bad habit on my part. But if I can be said to have to come to any—even tentative—conclusion, it might be this: we are trying to create a society that people want, but at the same time we're trying to influence their desires through discussion and education. I'm not quite sure you could call this a paradox, but it's definitely a balancing act. How much to listen and how much to lead? We might never get the balance precisely right, but we must never stop trying.

I wish you luck in the finishing of your book and hope you might one day have the opportunity to visit us again.

Until then.

As I do each and every day, I'm listening back to the tapes. The tapes that—I believed at that time and still believe to a certain extent—will inform and shape the material for this book. The tape I start listening back to is actually one of the interviews I remember most vividly. We were hiking on the mountain. In the background are all the sounds of our hike: our boots on the leaves and twigs and underbrush, small animals and insects and the wind. Listening back, I'm not sure I can identify any of these individual sounds, but the audio that surrounds and defines our voices is unquestionably more resonant and complex. What I remember most is my arm getting tired as it worked to steadily hold out the tape recorder in front of her, careful to keep pace, careful not to stumble on any obstacles or be so distracted by my task that I walked straight into a tree.

—Do you often come walking here?

—At least once a week. In good weather practically every other day. Sometimes I worry these walks are the only thing keeping me sane.

—Why is that a worry?

—I worry about stress. About the stress so many of us are under. What it's doing to us. What it's doing to our future.

—But walking like this through nature helps.

—How could it not? When people talk about war, they so often think only of human casualties or injuries or trauma. But what about how it affects the landscape, the animals, trees, and water? Everything around us is also terrorized by the violence.

—Those questions are usually framed around pollution and global warming and climate chaos.

—I know. Maybe all I'm saying is that it's all connected.

I remember how at this moment we both stopped. We had come to a plateau and the view was particularly stunning. From here you could look over the entire forest. Within the forest there had been a great deal of fighting. And you could even spot a few craters where stray bombs had felled the trees. But the forest was still thick, those trees would grow back, and listening to the silence on the tape crackle with background wildlife I remembered us standing side by side, taking in the landscape as fully as possible. It would be nice to be back there now.

—What do you think about on your walks?

—I try not to think too much. Mostly just take in my surroundings. To see every tree and pebble and insect. To feel how it all interrelates. How all these things need each other and none of them actually need us. How all of it would thrive so much more fully if we were gone.

—That sounds almost fatalist. Or nihilist.

—I don't think so. There is a kind of humility I find so important. Knowing human beings aren't actually the centre of anything. We've done considerable damage thinking we're the centre of the world.

—Why is that damaging?

—Because when you're the centre of the world, you can do whatever you want. The world revolves around you. And we're not the centre of anything. We're just full of ourselves.

As we stood there quietly inhaling the view, I tried to have some thoughts about the landscape that spread out in front of us. There was a forest and a river. At least, when you looked in this direction there was a forest and a river. I knew if we snaked our way around to the other side of the mountain the view would be rocks and hills and ridges. Dirt and sand. I didn't know enough about geology to hazard a guess as to why one side was so lush and green and the other was not. I was about to ask a question along these lines when my thoughts were interrupted.

—I don't know if I want this on the record. But since you're recording me anyway, I guess I won't object.

—If you like I can stop recording.

163

—No, it's all right. Maybe it's good that you have a record of what I'm about to say.

There is a long pause. So long that I wonder if the tape recorder had stopped working, but the background sounds of the mountain assure me the tape is still rolling.

—What is it you want to say?

—What I want to say is that I simply don't like the fact that you're here. It doesn't sit well with me.

—I'm sorry to hear that.

I remember the tension in my body as I braced myself for whatever she was about to say. Whatever it was, I was sure there would be a great deal of truth to it, that I would largely agree with her arguments. I was there to learn, and unfortunately that also included learning more of the reasons why I should have never ended up there in the first place.

—You're going to write about us, but you're never going to get it right. I can feel that just from the way you are in the world. But that's not it, that's not quite what I mean. Whatever you write might not do us much good, but from what I can tell, you're sincere enough, so it probably also won't do much harm. It's really something else, I'm not even sure I can fully articulate it.

—I'm listening. Don't worry, I can take it.

—I'm definitely not worried about hurting your feelings.

—Why not?

—Any of us here, all of us, we might be killed any day now, any minute. Our lives are what matters. In this context your feelings definitely don't matter.

—The criticism I've already received is that I'm only a tourist here, I have no real commitment to this place. I'm not invested enough.

—That's certainly true.

—But that's not what you're trying to tell me. You want to say something else.

—You want to learn from us but you can't because it's always going to be about you. I don't know why exactly. And I don't even want to know why. But that's the way that I see it. That's what I see.

—You're probably right. So what I should do is leave?

—Yes, you should leave.

But of course I didn't leave right away. I think that mountainside conversation was maybe five or six weeks before I went out on my first patrol, which as we now know resulted in my capture and interrogation. And I remember how I spent those five or six weeks thinking she was right, that I should leave now. That now was really the time to go—what was I waiting for? I often say that when I don't know what to do I become paralyzed, but here was a situation where even when I did know what to do I found myself paralyzed. I knew I couldn't stay but neither could I get myself to start leaving. It went on like that for week after week after week. The tape continued.

—I understand what you're saying.

—That's the thing. You understand. You can leave. But do you also understand that I can't?

—You can't leave because this is your home. This is your home and you have to stay here and fight for it?

—You really have a romantic idea of us, don't you?

—I'm sorry. Tell me. Why can't you leave?

—I can't leave because I have no money. No passport. No way to get anywhere. No other country that would take me in.

—But do you want to leave?

—I want the freedom you take for granted. All the freedoms. The freedom to walk up this mountain and know it's my home, to know it will survive, and also the freedom to tomorrow be on a tropical beach and forget this war for as long as I choose, until I recover, until I'm ready to come back to it. It's not that I would actually get on a plane and go anywhere. Perhaps quietly walking up this mountain once a week is enough for me. But why can't I have that freedom? Just to know it's possible, just to know that I can. And then it sounds like this is about me, or about you, but it has nothing to do with me or you. Some people can go wherever they want, and others can't, and it's the worst bullshit I've ever heard. Maybe that's really what I'm getting at. Some people can go wherever they want, meaning you can also pick up and come here, no one will stop you, we even welcome you with open arms. Because we're not stupid. We also know you have access that we don't so easily have. More of a voice on the world stage. But what we have to say, what we're actually living, is so clearly more important than anything you will ever write. And it fucking sucks that you have more of a voice than us. It's bullshit and it fucking sucks, but that's the way the world is, for now at least, and therefore the only thing me telling you all this actually does is give me a chance to vent and complain.

I remember the feeling of standing there on the mountainside, looking over the endless expanse of forest, her voice as she told me: "You're going to write about us but you're never going to get it right." And once again it makes me realize how never in my life as a writer have I genuinely tried to get anything "right," if getting it right means an accurate portrayal of reality, or even if it means providing access to something we might call truth or wisdom. In fact, it now seems to me, I have attempted to do almost the opposite, a search for how to "get it wrong" as evocatively as possible. Or to fully engage in the struggle between getting it right and getting it wrong. Of course, I'm always considering ethics, so I would never want to be ethically wrong, or to harm anyone with my words, but nonetheless there is the desire to be artistically off-kilter in ways that create the possibility of seeing things anew. To fully admit that I don't know. But now I'm not so sure. Rethinking all such assumptions might be one of the many ways I find myself trying to change.

A few days later I see a photocopied poster for a talk that will be given the following week, a talk by a representative from the thin strip of land. There is a grainy photograph of her next to her name. I stare at the poster for a long time but don't think I recognize her. I'm quite sure she wasn't someone I met during my time there. When I arrive it's a classroom at a community centre, thirty or forty folding chairs in rows facing a whiteboard at the front of the room. I recognize a few people. We smile hello. Top 40 music is playing quietly in the background, and I recognize the song, a song from the eighties I used to hear all the time but now had forgotten about. (I don't think they had any other hits. I've always been fascinated by one-hit wonders, what their life must be like, having most likely made so much music but only to be known for that one song.) All in all, there aren't a lot of us here, most of the folding chairs remain empty. All I can think is how depressing. My time on the thin strip of land was the most inspiring experience of my life, but now that I'm back home only a smattering of people can be bothered to come hear about it. The talk starts almost forty-five minutes late, because they keep hoping a few extra people might show up and therefore decide to wait and then wait a little bit more. Five minutes and then another five minutes. Wait and repeat. It seems the organizers are as disappointed with the low turnout as I am. When it does finally start, the mood in the room shifts and I'm suddenly excited. It feels like something is happening, there is a quality of attention letting me know I am not the only one who cares—everyone here seems to know how important this is. The talk has barely started and already I feel a little bit less alone.

And now I face a question I have faced many times over the course of this book. As she walks to the front of the room and we all watch her, waiting for her first words in complete anticipation, I start thinking about how I'm going to describe her. More importantly, what name will I use? Should I use her real name? Now that I'm home, perhaps it's time to start using real names again. For some reason, I decide against this. There might be no danger, but nonetheless it seems best to continue what I started, just in case, or because it's already become a bad habit. I briefly consider an allegorical name such as "fighter" but then realize how much I hate writers who attempt to pull off that kind of shit. Finally, several weeks later, I settle on the name Zasulich, after the Russian writer and revolutionary Vera Zasulich, who I admit I know relatively little about.

Zasulich begins by thanking us all for coming, then apologizes that she won't be showing any images tonight. Her computer stopped working a few hours ago, she's not sure why. I was disappointed. I had been hoping to see photographs of the places and people who had meant so much to me. Visual triggers for a complex array of memories. She continues by saying she was not going to ask us for money. She considered the talk she was about to give to be part of a larger world of such talks, a genre if you will, and this genre almost always ended with a plea for money and support. Of course, the situation she was going to tell us about required resources, actually could use all the help they could get, but that was not why she wanted to talk to us here tonight. If we were interested in anything like that, we could do the research and find the proper channels ourselves. She wanted to talk to us about something quite different. About what it was like to have ideals, to collectively nurture them over time and then attempt the larger challenge of putting those ideals into practice. Most of us here tonight, in this room, would have our own ideals, small and large. Some of those ideals it was possible to put into practice in our daily lives, in how we lived. But the larger the ideals, the more collective agreement was required to bring them into reality.

Their own collective undertaking—which all of us must

at least know a little about or we wouldn't be here in the first place—was made possible by an accident of fate, or at least of chance. Surrounded by war, their government collapsed and fled, providing them with an opportunity to take over, an opportunity they had been preparing for since long before she was born. Suddenly the land was theirs and they could do as they pleased, and all at once there were so many things to figure out, so many questions to answer. When she says they had been preparing for a long time, she also had to explain that not everyone had been involved in such preparations. Almost two million live there, and yet only a few hundred, maybe more like a thousand, had been involved in formulating and refining these ideas for the society in which they someday hoped to live. So what to do? When she tells the story like this, using such broad strokes, it feels to her almost like a fairy tale. A small group of outcasts who had, for years, been teaching themselves to make candles in semi-secret. No one wants their candles. This is the electric age, we have light bulbs and flashlights now. Then, suddenly, out of nowhere, the sky goes dark, all electricity ceases to work, and the world enters into an endless night. As people begin to grow agitated, as they begin to panic, our band of outcasts calmly walk through the centre of town with their candles lit, and by candlelight fix the generator, then teach others to make candles. Together, in candlelight, they all get to work. Of course, it was not really like that. This is merely the ideal toward which they strived. So what was it like in reality? This is what she has come here to tell us.

But before she did, there was one more thing she would be remiss in not attempting to explain, which had to do with the reason, the why—why she felt it important to convey what it was like. And this why had to do with our situation here and now, in the so-called free world. It might seem like things would just keep on going forever in the way they always had. But that was exactly how it had seemed to them back when they were quietly, in their corner, making their candles that no one wanted. (They were not actually making candles, but she'll continue with the analogy for now.) They didn't predict that the government would collapse and flee. They had, in fact, assumed the opposite: that the government would become more oppressive and eventually they would need to put their program into place using force. (Which would require a lot more than candles.) So just as we might not see any immediate opportunities for substantial change—for a significant paradigm shift—in how our society currently operates, they also didn't see any immediate opportunities. But nonetheless the opportunity arose.

And then the strange thing happened. She said she had come here to tell us what it was like, what it was like to live your ideals and experience a revolution, but she couldn't tell us. There was no way to say it. She could never quite find the words. There were no words. She wanted to inspire us, but that would also be the worst possible thing she could do, or at least she didn't know how. I realized that over the course of her talk her tone had gotten consistently more uncertain and was now more enwrapped in a freefall of hesitations, ill-timed pauses, and uncertainty than it was in the task of giving a talk. I wondered if she was having a nervous breakdown right there in front of us. As she continued, her voice seemed to hang on its last frayed nerve: "There are no words. Or maybe there are words, someone else has the words, but I don't have them. I give many of these talks, of this particular genre of talk, and each time I do my best to paint a picture, make it full and alive and rich. But I don't want to do that anymore. Actually I just can't. What I came here to tell you is something I can't do. I hope you understand. I have no more candles and no one wants candles here anyway. What would you do with a candle? Put it on a fucking birthday cake? I think you know what I mean."

Those of us sitting in the folding chairs were by this point all glancing nervously at one another, not knowing if one of us should intervene. Or if the organizers should. It was hard to find a moment to do so or figure out how it should be done. Zasulich was standing in front of us, almost hovering, lost in a pause so long we thought maybe she had come to the end, but then she began again: "You know that feeling when you have something you want to say but mainly you just don't want to? I think we all know what I mean. It's a question of words, of having or not having the right words. And I no longer have them. And anyway, now is not the right time for words. Now is the time for action. Or maybe not now but when the time comes. Someone has to know. Doesn't someone have to know? I came here to give a talk. You can't come somewhere to give an action. But if I could I would. Thanks for having me and thanks for your time."

She then walked offstage, so to speak, walked directly to the back corner of the room, and then stood there in the corner, as if there was no escape, as if there was nowhere else for her to go. We all applauded nervously. Two of the organizers rushed to her side to comfort her, make sure she was all right, take care of her, while a third stepped to the front of the room, said that normally at this juncture they would take questions, but considering the circumstances, if we all agreed, they would forgo the questions in this particular instance. Of course we agreed, quietly nodding our assent. But no one left. We all sat there in a kind of mute, stunned silence. I didn't know if it was all right for me to feel this way, because I didn't know if Zasulich was okay, but nonetheless I felt that what we had all just experienced together was so much more powerful than a normal talk, and certainly more unnerving and compelling than any talk I had ever before experienced. But it wasn't exactly on purpose, these effects, which made it difficult to know how one should think or feel in response. And she was right: there were no words.

Everyone remains seated, but slowly, gently, they begin to talk with one another from their seats. The three organizers surround Zasulich in the back corner, but the situation seems to have calmed down so—not sure if it's the right thing to do—I decide it can't hurt to wander over and introduce myself. Surprisingly, she has already been given my name as someone she should look up when she came to town. She seems more or less back to normal now, relaxed and down-to-earth. She tells me she hasn't been back to the thin strip of land in over five years. She believes that if she goes back, there is a very great likelihood that when she enters any of the neighbouring countries, she'll be detained. (And there is no other way to get there, since the thin strip of land has no airport of its own and is landlocked.) So she has to do whatever she can from afar. She gives about fifty of these talks each year and clearly it's taking its toll, she knows this, she has to slow down, find another way to go about things, to get the message out. Since she's not sure anymore, what can you really say: We're doing the revolution, give us money, thank you for your time. It all seems so empty and self-serving. She asks if she can tell me something personal and I say that she can. She got a message earlier that morning that her brother had stepped on a land mine and blown off his leg. She hasn't seen him in such a long time. That is probably the real reason for her current mental state. Is it really right for her to be so far away from the action? She knows it isn't, but should she risk an attempt to go home? She could do more for the revolution alive than dead.

She didn't know why she was telling me all this. She received the news this morning, she needed to tell someone, and I was the first person to introduce myself. She hoped I didn't mind. I told her it was more than all right, and if she wanted to talk, I was more than willing to listen. We agree to meet the following day, exchange contact information, decide on a time and place. Moments later she's whisked away by the three organizers as we say a much-too-quick goodbye. I look around the room. While I've been talking to Zasulich, everyone else has left. An empty room with a few rows of folding chairs staring at me in judgment. One by one I fold each chair and rest it against the wall. When all the chairs are folded, I quietly leave, closing the door behind me.

The next day I get to the café too early. I sip my coffee and think about my life, wondering if she will actually show up. There is a song playing over the sound system that I can't quite place. I'm not sure if it's a song from the eighties or a song from now that sounds like it was recorded in the eighties. There are many songs now that fit this particular description. As I sit there, I listen to many songs. I try reading a book but find I can't concentrate. I try taking notes for this book but don't have any particular new ideas. After about three hours, during which I also consume many coffees, one sandwich, and one pastry, I come to the sad conclusion that she's not going to show. I'm disappointed but at the same time almost relieved. As I'm slowly walking home, I think again about Zasulich's talk. I had never seen anyone fall apart like that in front of an audience, even if we were such a small crowd. It was so vulnerable, so unnerving. Was she all right, and if she wasn't what could I do?

During this time, I also attempted to come up with an explanation as to why the planes were exploding. I thought that would be a good way to end this book, with an explanation. I did not succeed. Much like why men so often go to war, it might be a mystery that will never be solved. But I've always known at least one reason: where there's war, there is money to be made. (It was around this time that I read that to operate the Guantánamo Bay prison, it costs $11 million per prisoner per year. That means more than $30,000 a day for each prisoner. I am now back home, no longer detained, but horrifically those in Guantánamo remain incarcerated at the psychotic cost of $30,000 per day.) Of course, "terrorists" are continuously being blamed for blowing up the planes. But there is no proof. And for some reason the media, the politicians, and the status quo have had trouble making this narrative stick. If it was terrorists, they would only be blowing up *our* planes, but planes from all countries and factions seem to explode at basically the same rate. What kind of terrorists would work in this way? Terrorists who were against all war and bombing, which makes no sense. Terrorists for peace.

What a society decides to do, what a society actually does, what a society chooses to spend its money on, over time becomes the truth of that society. We can choose to help people or we can choose to kill, and you only have to look closely at the national budget to see how we've made our choice. If the entirety of the military budget was put to different ends, the mind boggles at what might be achieved: an end to hunger, an end to poverty, an environmental revolution, a resurgence of the natural world, proper health care to effectively deal with future pandemics, a chance for so much suffering to be lessened and transformed. We know this already. We know this, but how can I make you truly feel it? And are such feelings even where the solution lies? So much needs to change, right down to our fundamental understanding of what it means to live. I often ask myself if I've really even taken the first step.

The letter from Zana

I have been thinking a great deal about compost. I believe you already know enough about me to know that this is not surprising. I know you are the writer. You are the one who lives from metaphors and analogies and all of that. Who is in the business of words. I don't care for metaphors. I am concerned with practical matters, with finding things that work in the real-life world. Because I have to be if there is any chance that our experiment here will survive, but also because that's who I am. That's, of course, not who you are. We are very different from each other. It is good that the world is full of such different people, it keeps things interesting. Nonetheless, I think you know what I'm trying to say. You basically say it about yourself in the manuscript, many times and in many different ways, and therefore probably don't need to hear it again from me. You already know. That's also the problem, you already know. Self-awareness without change. For me this is the underlying theme of the manuscript you have sent us and so gently asked us to read. It is not a theme I can get behind or even find myself particularly interested in. So against your theme, I bring a theme of my own.

Soil is not a metaphor. Compost is not a metaphor. In depleted soil very little can grow. But depleted soil is rarely the end of the story. With enough time, attention, and care, basically all soil can be replenished. And things can then grow again. This is not a metaphor, but writing to you it seems impossible for me to avoid the temptation of using it as such. So then what is it a metaphor for? (Once again you can sense my desire to put everything toward practical use.) For people? For society? For our emotional inner lives? If anything, I might choose to see it as an analogy for the world view we are raised within, for how we collectively choose to see the world. I'm sure I'm not the first person to make these connections. Plants grow in seasons. They grow, are harvested, lay dormant, then grow once again. They don't just keep growing and growing forever, ceaselessly and without rest. In permaculture we plant the different crops all on the same plot, close together, so they can form symbiotic relationships and help each other. We don't do this randomly. We do so based on our observations, over time. Which plants like each other, how do they help each other coexist? Compost is full of things that are normally thrown away, that are normally thought of as garbage or waste, and yet when gathered together, with the proper attention and tending, it can be used to take depleted soil and over time transform it into something fertile and necessary. What are you throwing away that might instead be used to transform your life into something more useful?

What I know is true, but your manuscript fails to convey, is that the world is shifting underneath our feet as we speak. It might change for the worse or might change for the better, probably a bit of both, but it's definitely not going to continuously stagnate and remain the same. And that is perhaps the only criticism I truly wish to convey: that reading your book doesn't make me feel how all things are alive and full of change. Living here on this thin strip of land does. It's certainly unfair to compare your book to my life, but due to your manuscript's subject matter, at the same time how can I possibly not?

I'm thinking back to a moment we shared together, a moment that is also in your book, when you asked me if you should move here with us, move onto a farm here and spend the rest of your life tending the soil. And I didn't take you seriously, said you would never be happy if you did. You told me you were already unhappy, so why not split the difference. If I were to have that conversation again now, I might respond differently. Tell you, why not, move here to farm and see how long you last. Work to learn our language so you can be here more fully. Maybe ten or twenty years of farming and then let's see what kind of book you would write. It would be an interesting experiment. As you know, here on the thin strip of land, we like to think of life as an experiment. You change the way you do something and then later talk about how it went, analyze the results, figure out together what further changes you hope to try. I like this way of thinking about our time here in the world. Trial and error, learn from our mistakes and cherish our successes. That might be the best note to leave you on. I don't think I've been particularly harsh toward your work in this letter, but if I was, please know that wasn't my intention. Because I do see that you do, at least at times, learn from your mistakes. So perhaps the cherishing of your successes is still to come.

My life these days is so boring. I listen to the tapes, transcribe them, struggle to make continued progress on this book. Back when I was on my ill-advised journey, each day felt so dangerous and strange, but now that I'm home, it all, once again, feels routine and mundane. I know I have no one to blame but myself. The daily life of a writer is often not so compelling to live or read about. But the other day, as part of the introduction to Zasulich's talk, there was an announcement of a demonstration. I wrote down the details and now find myself preparing to go. In the past I've often avoided large demonstrations. Though I believe in them politically, I don't necessarily like the feeling of being part of a large crowd. Or that was the old me, and I'm still dreaming of a new me that finds it easier to get involved.

I'm several blocks away, but already I can hear them chanting. The moment I hear them I begin to cry. I'm not completely sure why. I suppose I just find it moving, hearing so many people coming together to fight for a cause. When I arrive at the square it's packed, wall-to-wall people, a much larger demonstration than I was expecting. I'm about to begin the long process of pushing my way into the middle of the crowd when, over in the corner, I spot Zasulich with the three organizers from the other night. I'm not sure if I should leave her alone—she didn't come to our meeting so perhaps that means she'd rather be free of me—but curiosity gets the better of me as I find myself carefully weaving through the crowd. When Zasulich sees me she immediately gives me a big hug, which I find surprising since we barely know each other, and while we're hugging she apologizes several times for missing our meeting. I wouldn't believe the difficult week she's had, difficult is an understatement. She was arrested for being here illegally and it took her friends, she says, gesturing toward the three organizers, a full week to get her back out. She was not here illegally, all her papers were in order, she had even been granted political asylum, but to convince them of this fact was a convoluted, labyrinthine, bureaucratic process that would have made even Kafka blush. She would have sent a message, but they took her phone, and her computer still doesn't work, though that barely matters because they took her computer as well. The three organizers watch her hugging me with bemusement, nodding along to confirm the details of her story. She then said there was another thing she wanted to tell me. When she told her friends back home that she was coming here to give a talk, they not only suggested she look me up, they also told her about my manuscript. It took a while, but eventually one of the many copies that were circulating on the thin strip of land made its way back to her, and she had the time to read it during her brief stay in jail. (They wouldn't let her have a phone or a pen, but they did let her keep the crumpled pile of photocopies, and that was the one saving grace of the entire experience.) She wanted to talk to me about it. She had so many thoughts and questions. She also wondered if she should write her own book, if I might be willing to help her, and then maybe we could go about promoting our books together.

We were no longer hugging by this point, and my thoughts could barely keep up. I was struggling to process everything she had told me. It had been a while since I had received so much new information all at once. When she hadn't shown up for our meeting I assumed she'd changed her mind, no longer wanted to meet—what other reason could there possibly be? It would have never occurred to me that she'd been arrested. If it had I would have done something, gone to visit her, met with the organizers to see if there was anything I could do to help. Or would I? I'm not sure.

That doesn't particularly sound like me either. Behind us the demonstration grows more heated and raucous. In the distance we hear sirens, and Zasulich says that maybe we should slip away. Normally she would be up for a fight, for any sort of confrontation, but having just been released from jail earlier that day she wasn't sure she wanted to go back so soon. Maybe this time they wouldn't be able to get her out again. Or she'd be sent back home, which, she now thought, might be the best possible thing that could happen to her. But if it wasn't, she wasn't sure she wanted to find out the hard way. And she wasn't sure she wanted to find out tonight.

The five of us all end up going for dinner. By the time we get to the restaurant, Zasulich has calmed down, gone quiet, and the three organizers and I do most of the talking. They tell me how they've been working to raise awareness about the struggles taking place on the thin strip of land, how difficult it is to get any coverage in mainstream media, and even when the coverage comes it is often skewed toward a more conventional telling of the story: feminist women fighting foreign bad guys, leaving aside all the emancipatory political experiments that are, of course, the most inspiring part. They're amazed I've actually been there, repeatedly ask me what it's like, and I do my best to describe it but feel disappointed in my retelling, wish there was a way to make my description of it more vivid and evocative. The organizers don't seem to mind. They're so interested in hearing anything I can tell them, and in their interest and curiosity I'm once again able to see the fascination of it all.

After we've eaten, Zasulich perks up again, comes back to life, rejoining the conversation. She says that in jail, even though it was only a week, she had time to think. Also, she didn't know it would only be a week. There were days she thought she might be in there for a very long time. She thought about her life here and how different it was from her life back home. And in the end there was really only one difference: back home the people she was surrounded by were people she had been living and fighting alongside for her entire life. She knew them like her own soul. And if she looked around this table, at each of us, no offence, but we were all basically strangers. She appreciated everything we were doing for the cause, but that didn't change the fact that we were strangers. That wasn't the whole story—maybe it wasn't even true anymore. Because, yes, when she lived on the thin strip of land, she was surrounded by people she had known her entire life. But that was over five years ago, and those five years now make up a significant portion of her life. What will it be like when it's ten or fifteen years? How will that feel? Because so much of her time here had been spent travelling and giving talks, which often meant being a stranger, and being surrounded by relative strangers, being a guest of the organizations that so generously hosted her. Of course, she had friends in her new life, close friends, both from here and from the diaspora of her homeland, but it wasn't the same, it was never as close, it was never life or death, that closeness that came from relying on each other, from being under threat, defending themselves together. She wasn't sure why she was telling us all this. She wasn't sure exactly what she was trying to say. Maybe only that she was afraid she was already starting to live in the past. Even as the past was receding, growing farther and farther away from her current life experience. Something she no longer lived but instead gave talks about. Even though she had to keep giving these talks. It was so important to keep spreading the word.

The four of us sat there and listened, fascinated by her conundrum but also worried for her mental health. The conversation turned toward how else she could be doing it, the pros and cons of various approaches, if there was a way she could continue spreading the word that would be easier for her to bear. The possibility emerged that she could make a documentary or a radio show or content for the Internet, bringing her back around to the idea that she would write a book. That reading my manuscript was interesting enough, but there should also be another book by someone who had been there from the very beginning, someone who had truly lived it. A book written from within the struggle and not by an outsider. We were all enthusiastic about this idea, offered encouragement. As we were saying our goodbyes, I again agreed to help her write it and get it published. Whatever help she needed. I promised.

There was only one letter left in the package. I hesitate before reading it. I know, after I read it, there will be no more. This is my last more current link to my time on the thin strip of land, to the people I met there. Of course, I can continue listening to the cassettes, but they are receding into the past. These letters are more recent. Several days pass as I stare at the final letter sitting on my desk. I want to read it while at the same time I don't, like slowing down as you reach the final pages of a book you are reading, when you don't want it to end. But I couldn't wait forever. Sooner or later I had to tear it open and find out what it said.

The letter from an anonymous student

You probably won't remember me. You came to our classroom to tell us about being a writer. I was sitting at the back of the class. You took questions, but I didn't ask any. I just sat there and observed, took it all in, the absurdity of the situation, of you being there and how awkward it was. Nonetheless, your talk did make an impression on me. Even though I agreed with almost nothing you said. Disagreeing with you helped me formulate my own thinking. Which also helped me formulate something I'm not sure I understood up until that moment: that it's not useful to be surrounded only by like-minded people, or even by people with the same history as you. (Almost everyone I know here has spent their life on the same territory and within the same situation.) That it is also important to be confronted by someone with a different perspective. Someone who comes from another place. I am still quite young, so in all likelihood, sooner or later I would have met other people and come to this realization in another way. But it wasn't someone else, it was you, and therefore I thought a good way to begin this letter would be to tell you this personal fact.

And then a friend told me there were copies of your manuscript going around, that you had sent a few copies to us, and others had made copies of those copies, I'm not sure how many there are now, but a classmate was reading it and I asked them if I could read it next. It might be worth mentioning that the copy I read was extremely tattered, it had clearly passed through many hands, with passages so smudged I found them difficult to decipher. This gave me the feeling that I was reading something illicit, something a bit secret, even though there are no rules here as to what one is or isn't allowed to read. The tattered quality of the pages certainly gave a certain frisson to my reading experience. I think this was quite different than if I had read it in the form of a published book.

I don't want to focus so much on the part about us. Everyone always wants to talk about themselves. I see this as a weakness. The very fact that you write about us is flattering, and the way you write about us is flattering as well. But I don't want to be seduced and I don't want to be flattered. Our struggle here is real. It doesn't need your approval or attention to make it any more real. As I think you already know, the truth of our event is something we'll have to continue to figure out for ourselves.

I would prefer to focus on the other two sections. The chapter before you get here and the chapter just after you leave. They are sections where you are mostly alone, and I believe you are trying to tell the world that it is not good to be too alone, but the world already knows that. Or that being too alone makes you politically impotent. But I was in that classroom where I first encountered you because I too want to be a writer. When I write I sit in a room alone to do so. Right now I am sitting alone in my room writing you this letter. And I don't think this writerly loneliness makes me any more politically impotent than anyone else. I realize our situations are different, but they are not as different as you might at first think. Yes, I am here experiencing a revolution in real time, but that doesn't mean I naturally know how to write about it, or what I might write that would be most useful for our struggle. I need to work to figure it out in the same way you do. My lived experience doesn't magically grant me the truth. But it does provide a certain freedom, a freedom that feels like breathing and moving and having the room to make mistakes—not only in my body but also in my mind; not only in my mind but also in my body—and a freedom that, yes, feels like being considerably less alone. When I write I try to embody and encompass this multilinear feeling of freedom.

Reading your manuscript I thought often of our enemies. Our enemies believe they are disciplined and strong while we are undisciplined and weak. They see their right to rule and fight and dominate as a natural extension of their strength and character. Behind this position, one suspects, is an entire universe of insecurity and self-doubt. But what if this analysis is wrong? What if they are simply shallow and self-confident in their absolute expression of violence? But that is not really what I'm getting at. Instead I wanted to ask you something else. If our enemies think we are undisciplined and weak, how does your constant literary expression of your own misguided weakness, your own constantly being wrong, play into their hands? They say we're weak and wrong, and you also say you're weak and often wrong, so what does it do to agree with our enemies so completely?

I realize this is a strange question to ask. Because, in fact, you posit your own weakness, not in contrast to our enemies, but in contrast to us. (Us here on the thin strip of land.) You are weak but we are strong. You don't know how to fight but we do. But is the reader supposed to identify with you—you are, after all, the protagonist of your own book—or is the reader supposed to identify with us? Or a bit of both? What I am trying to ask, and there might be no answer to this question, is: What literary purpose does your self-imposed, self-reflexive weakness actually serve? Can you see how it might play so directly into the enemy's hands, into their own narrative regarding their natural superiority over you? Can you see how it might be self-defeating not only in an insightfully literary sense, but in a political one as well?

And then I understand another reality about what you are trying to do. You are trying to be honest: about yourself, about your character, about your place and role in the world. I like honesty as much as the next writer. But this desire for honesty leads me to question you even further: Are you certain you're being honest with yourself? Because underneath your self-confessed weakness and monumental doubt, I sense an equally monumental ego that expresses itself through the very desire to continue writing books. So instead of always questioning whether these books are as politically effective and useful as you might want them to be, why not believe in yourself more, put your disowned ego to better use by owning it more, and work on whatever rhetorical efficacy is necessary to make your books as politically helpful and potent as possible? I feel this suggestion is almost the exact opposite of everything you believe in and stand for, which is the reason I make it. Just as, when I first encountered you in that classroom, you helped me confront the limitations of my own ideas by bringing them into conflict with your ideas—ideas that were at the time so different and counterintuitive for me. I would now like to do the same for you. This might not be as easy, because of our age difference. I am relatively young and therefore still experiencing a lot of ideas for the first time. You are not so young anymore and therefore must find it harder to feel that you are experiencing something new, must often feel you've heard it all before. But if there's one thing I know about pedagogy, it's that it can only be worthwhile if the teacher is also able to learn from the student. Which I suppose is the main reason I now find myself writing this letter to you.

And why, in those chapters I'm examining here, do you keep saying, "This book is not reality"? Don't you see how it erases us, how it discounts our lived experience? As I said before, our struggle is real. Just because you prefer to write fiction doesn't mean you must discount or dismiss the real. Or that you can afford not to believe in reality as you write. Yes, take freedom as you write, but listen to the freedom as I describe it, as we are living it here, the freedom of breathing and moving and having the room to make mistakes and being considerably less alone. I believe this freedom is not only for us here on the thin strip of land. I believe, or at least hope, that it can be created anywhere. By coming together and finding strength in doing so. And this is the place from which I hope to be a writer—now still a young writer but I won't always be this young. This is the place from which I hope to continue to write, and in telling you this, I don't think you'll be surprised to hear that I suggest you might learn to do the same.

I hope you take these thoughts in the generous and helpful spirit with which they are intended. Maybe one day we'll meet at a literary festival or something. By the time I publish my first book, I hope to be at least that good.

Sincerely,

The letter is signed with a name I have never seen before. I sit there at my desk, holding the letter in my hands, not thinking anything, not doing anything, trying to take it all in. This was the last letter in the package. There were no more letters to look forward to, no more letters left to read. I had been put in front of a classroom and this was the response. I'm not sure I could have possibly hoped for more.

When I look back at the history of a certain kind of literature, I often see myself. In writers like Franz Kafka, Fernando Pessoa, Robert Musil, Robert Walser, Roberto Arlt, Sadegh Hedayat, Witold Gombrowicz, Cesare Pavese: depressed and mostly European literary melancholics— often published posthumously—who could do little other than write and whose writing fed their alienated melancholia and vice versa. It is telling that none of these writers ever attempted to write an anti-war novel. Many of them never even got on a plane. Sometimes I tell myself: now is the time to change. If I believe, with all the injustices that surround us, that activism in our current moment is more important than art, then I must step up, transform myself, be the change I wish to see. (Like Prince at the end of *Purple Rain*, except with politics.) Then I feel I'm only lying to myself, since if I am good at anything—and I'm not so sure I am—it will always have something to do with art, and therefore it is only through writing or art that I might make anything happen. So here I am, again trying to write this book. From my own all-too-flawed perspective. Having read all four letters from the thin strip of land and hoping their insights and criticisms continue to change the way I write and live. Once again unsure whether I'm doing right or wrong. And I remember this quote from an interview with the poet Myung Mi Kim: "The undecidability of whether I am making a difference or not—that ambiguity is part of the answer. Part of the work of answering the question of social efficacy has to include the ambiguity. If you actually had an answer, you wouldn't be taking in the whole full weight of the questions."

A few days later another thing happens that is not entirely unexpected but, at the same time, *is* entirely unexpected (at least at that specific juncture). The world market for oil collapses. When I was living on the thin strip of land, I was worried that sooner or later they would be invaded for their oil. But now, quite suddenly, that possibility seems considerably less likely. I'm certainly not an economist and have only a rudimentary knowledge of speculation and the stock market, so my explanation of what occurred might be less than complete. But I will do my best.

When the world market for oil collapsed, to put it a bit simply, some countries were in the process of preparing for such an eventuality and others were clearly not. The country I lived in was extremely unprepared. Predictably enough, travel of any kind, especially long-distance travel, became difficult. (I could still ride my bicycle to get where I had to go.) The stock market crashed. Companies declared bankruptcy. Stocks for renewables such as wind and solar quickly skyrocketed. I don't believe in green capitalism, and certainly don't think anything so innocent happened as the market correcting itself, since the market was in a complete nervous breakdown, but something was happening that involved capital at its very core. Much like during other Great Depressions, many who lost their life savings committed suicide. Many of the front-page newspaper stories concerned such spectacular details. I read everything I could, wondering if this was the moment we'd been waiting for, a paradigm shift in the way markets organize themselves around resources.

A continuous stream of newspaper stories focused on different sites of resource extraction that were shutting down or on hiatus. Sucking oil from the ground was suddenly no longer profitable, or at least startlingly less so, and no one wanted to continue losing money at that rapidly accelerating rate, in ways that so deeply went against the current economic zeitgeist. However, no matter how much I read, perhaps because my grasp of the underlying economics was not thorough enough, I never completely understood what had happened to trigger this economic tailspin. Over the past few years, massive protests against—and sabotage of—pipelines had been on the rise, making business as usual ever more difficult to maintain. To what degree had protest and sabotage made this collapse and emancipatory opportunity occur? Public opinion had already turned ages ago; almost no one could now say, with a straight face, that oil has a secure place as part of humanity's future. So—at least this I think I correctly understand—when everyone started pulling their money out, everyone else started to panic and follow suit. I thought back to my time walking through the war. So many of the wars fought during my lifetime and before were fought over oil or similar resources, or more specifically the price of oil and similar resources, though those giving the orders would often not admit to this. (I knew wars in the future would most likely be fought over water, but that was yet to come.)

I was scheduled to meet with Zasulich again the next day, to discuss how we would approach working on her book together, but again she didn't show up. I thought: She couldn't have possibly gotten arrested again, not so soon. But anything was possible. I tried phoning, emailing, and texting her, all to no avail. I berated myself for not getting contact information from any of the three organizers when we all had dinner together. There was no one else I could call. I had also wanted to talk to Zasulich about oil. At that moment I wanted to talk to anyone and everyone about oil, anyone who would listen. I felt the current crisis was an opportunity, but I wasn't sure what kind of opportunity exactly, or how we could seize it. I was sure Zasulich would have ideas. After a tedious three-hour wait, reminiscent of my last three-hour wait in the exact same café, I began the long, meandering walk back to my apartment. It reminded me how when I was young I used to walk aimlessly for hours, not knowing what I was going to do with my life, if I would be a writer or a filmmaker or an activist, and if I were to become an activist what causes would I end up fighting for? Those youthful walks could last for hours, a notebook under my arm, perhaps hoping I would run into someone I knew but at the same time hoping I wouldn't, wondering if this was only what it was like to be young or if my life would always be like this. Tonight, I arrive back in front of my apartment but instead of going in decide to keep walking. There is so much for me to think about and walking has always been the best way for me to do so. I stop at a drinking fountain to refill my water bottle, and it reminds me of refilling the same water bottle from that well outside the abandoned village, the well that for a moment I worried might have been poisoned. Then I was worried about becoming paranoid and now I'm worried I'm becoming nostalgic.

I don't know how long I've been walking when my phone rings. It's Zasulich. She apologizes, first just wanting to assure me she's not once again in jail, but her life is complicated these days. There's a possibility her brother might try to come here for further medical treatment and she spent the entire day figuring out how to make that happen. It's not going to be easy. But in the process she forgot about our meeting. She once again apologizes and asks if I'm free to meet now. I'm not doing anything so I agree, change direction, and turn to walk back the same way I just came, over to the restaurant where Zasulich has suggested we meet.

As I walk, for no particular reason, I start thinking about my friend who met me at the airport when I got off the plane, realizing we hadn't been in touch for a while, which was most likely my fault. What might she have to say about all of this? About oil and Zasulich. When I first got back we wrote to each other a few times. She was angry I hadn't written sooner. She'd assumed I was long ago dead, and I felt so stupid and frustrated with myself for leaving her in the dark. But I apologized and apologized again and believe we eventually managed to patch things up. I should really write to her again soon, which got me thinking about how when we were both younger she would so often give me good advice and I would so rarely take it. That was such a long time ago, but how have I really changed? Can I promise myself now that if, in the future, someone gives me good advice I will listen as avidly as possible and, at the very least, try to do what they say? She gave me good advice about my trip, not to go, and once again I ignored her, just like old times, and yet if I had taken her advice I might have never met the people on the thin strip of land, which I'm certain will always be one of the most important experiences of my life. Then again, I hadn't given her all the necessary information, never even suggesting I was headed for the thin strip of land. I suppose I was too embarrassed by the naïveté of my endeavour. Perhaps if I'd filled her in on all the details, she would have given me different advice.

I'm getting closer to the restaurant, which means I should begin to mentally prepare for my meeting with Zasulich. What do I really want to tell her? That she should write her book. That I will do everything I can to help. That it's important she write her book. Do I really believe this? There are so many books in the world, what does it matter if there's one more or one less? But that's definitely not what I want to tell her. Because she has first-hand experience that so few of us will ever get to live. That experience needs to be shared, needs to be available for anyone who might want to make use of it. I know from my own experience that the best way to start writing a book is simply to start and that is what I will try to convey. That we can start right now. If she wants, together, in this restaurant, we can begin to write the first few paragraphs of the very first chapter. It won't be much, but nonetheless it's something we can do. I don't want to interfere with the content of her book but I do want to be a cheerleader for making it happen.

I now wasn't far from the restaurant, walking and day-dreaming as I always do, lost in these more hopeful

Afterword

It is ironic that after almost dying many times in my homeland, a place where—from my point of view—he was only
a tourist and had no particular right or necessity to be, my
friend—the author of this work—ended up dying several
blocks from his own apartment. Hit by an electric car. He
left this final book unfinished, as in a sense we all do, all of
our lives unfinished, since what could it possibly mean to
finish them?

Near the middle of this book he asks: "Is it possible to write
about my own death as if it were also the death of capitalism and patriarchy?" And strangely, in the unreal way he
has written up his travels, he in a sense does die four times,
once at the end of each section. Unfortunately this last time
was for keeps. Which makes me ask: Do capitalism and
patriarchy need to die or do they only need to change? (If
they change into something clearly unrecognizable as capitalism or patriarchy, do we say they changed or do we say
they died?) As we know, many people would rather die than
change and I'm still trying to figure out whether or not my
friend was one of them.

The decision to publish this book as it is, unfinished or not,
was not an easy one for his family or for the publisher. But
here we are. Perhaps for the publisher it was easier, since
I believe he had already spent his advance. As well, I am
sure, due to the surrounding circumstances, this book will
be met with a certain degree of anticipation and curiosity.

And so now I sit here, thinking of my friend, so recently gone, trying to formulate my approach to this rather peculiar task of writing an afterword for an unfinished book, a book that ends mid-sentence, a book that speaks as fiction of things that happened and didn't happen and every shade in between.

I believe the reason I have been asked to write this afterword is that I am ostensibly a character in this book. I know I am a character in this book. Or at least one of the characters is loosely based on me. I know I am a character, while at the same time I don't quite believe it. To be more specific, I am the unnamed friend who picks him up at the airport and later takes him to the "secret, illegal" party. As I contemplate writing this afterword, it occurs to me that even though I seem important enough throughout the opening pages, you learn almost nothing about me, or at least nothing about a fictionalized version of me. Therefore, I must admit, tragic circumstances aside, I feel almost a modicum of glee now being able to have the last word. When you've lived the life that I've lived, you honestly can't expect to have the last word very often. You expect to be a footnote in somebody else's last word. (As I, at times, felt when I was reading this book.) Therefore, along with providing the reader with whatever information is available to us as to the author's intentions, I will also do my best to sketch out my side of the story, that is to say: I will tell you how things really are.

Along with the chapters you've just read, the author, my friend, left behind a series of notes we can assume represent the material he considered including within the final pages. On his desk was a torn-out page from his first book. The following passage was highlighted:

And then I got an email advertising an art show, a show of photographs, photographs of all the places we have bombed since the end of World War Two: Cuba, Japan, China, Korea, Guatemala, Indonesia, Congo, Peru, Dominican Republic, Laos, Vietnam, Cambodia, Grenada, Lebanon, Puerto Rico, Libya, El Salvador, Nicaragua, Panama, Iraq, Sudan, Bosnia, Afghanistan and Yugoslavia.

He published that paragraph over twenty years ago. It perhaps gives insight into the original impetus for his trip and for then deciding to write this particular book in this particular way. (And we can now add to the list: Syria, Pakistan, Yemen, Somalia, and, by the time you read this, perhaps others.) Something we talked about many times is that if art or literature shows only that the world is awful, perhaps it is only adding to the awfulness rather than combatting it. I fondly remember those endless conversations we used to have about art and life and politics. By the time he visited me in my parents' old apartment, such youthful conversation seemed a million years away. As has already been mentioned earlier in this book, by that time I no longer thought of myself as an artist. The war, and perhaps also my parents' passing, washed all that away. However, he tells you I no longer produce works of art without telling you the new places that life has taken me. But we'll come back to that later.

You set out to write about what's wrong with the world— about war and bombing—but end up writing mostly about what's wrong with yourself. A side effect of having been raised in this culture in which individualism is continuously encouraged and, more to the point, of being engaged in a vocation, namely writing, in which one spends far too much time wrapped up in oneself and one's own thoughts. But perhaps I'm being too harsh. He does also tell us about all that is wrong with the world and then gives room for those on the thin strip of land to provide solutions. He was my friend and we never pulled our punches with each other, always held one another accountable. Those are qualities we both loved and admired in each other. I showed an earlier draft of this text to a few writer friends and they asked if I was aware it might seem harsh how cavalierly I've dismissed his death. But I think it's okay. We've had a lot of him already. We can end somewhere else. With something else. Since this is not a conventional book, it will also not be a conventional afterword. It is perhaps a bit shameless just how much I'm enjoying having the final word.

While preparing to write this, I spent a great deal of time with Zasulich. We became friends. She came and stayed with me for several months directly preceding her return to the thin strip of land. (It was touch and go there for a while, but she did, in the end, make it back home.) I assume you already know what the Bechdel test is. In an earlier draft of this afterword I recounted many of our conversations about this book's author, but then thought about the Bechdel test and deleted these sections, instead deciding to focus on other conversations and experiences. There was a café not far from my apartment, and Zasulich and I used to talk there together each morning. By this time the war had calmed down considerably and it was more possible to be out on the streets, still at times dangerous, but the desire for life to return to normal can never be suppressed for long. That café was where so many of our conversations occurred. Over time we told each other everything—long, winding, digression-filled confessions that brought us closer each and every time we picked up where we'd previously left off.

I learned that Zasulich was twenty when her territory was first liberated and how those years were among the best of her life. Everything still to be done, still to be figured out. It often brought me to thinking about my own formative years. How there's a certain period in your life when you're learning so much, so quickly. Zasulich seemed happy to be heading home. All the terror she might face there was, it seemed to me, less terrifying than the dislocation she had experienced abroad. I remember one morning at the café, she was telling me about a talk she'd given at one of the larger universities. How during the questions someone had asked why they should believe her. How could they be sure the society she was describing, and also asking money for, was actually as progressive and promising as she'd made it out to be. How at that moment it was like a bottomless void momentarily opened up underneath her. For a long, awkward silence she had absolutely no idea how to answer. They should believe her because she was telling the truth. But what proof could she give? What constituted a real truth in this world where everyone was trying to get money from everyone else? But she did answer in the end. She couldn't remember exactly what she'd said, but it was along the lines of: She could understand how someone could become cynical, about her or about anything else, but she had chosen not to, because in a way she had no choice. They were fighting for their lives, and in such a fight there is room for necessary self-questioning but no room for cynicism. Every day you must wake up and do the best you can. It's true she was asking for money, but if that's all he got from her talk, he'd missed the point. The point wasn't the money but the values they were fighting for. If they sometimes fell short of such values, that was no reason to give up, only to work harder in the future. Sitting in that café, listening to her explain all this to me, was complex in a way I'm not sure, even now, I'm able to fully explain. My life, especially the more recent part, had certainly been a struggle. But she was younger and it was clear she had struggled more. It certainly wasn't that she never got down. If that was true she wouldn't be here, sitting across from me, telling me about that suspicious audience member and his unfair question. She was here because her new life had been getting her down and she was trying to return to her old one, unsure she even could because of all the things that had changed on the thin strip of land in the time she'd been away. I felt in her some spark I worried I'd never had. (But was it too late? Could I still maybe find it?) The spark of having lived a communally built moment of ever-expanding freedom. I also worried I was romanticizing her. She was becoming a friend and I wanted to see her as a friend and not as a representative of any larger questions.

One morning when we were walking together to the café, she mentioned something about being happy to soon be on patrol again. To once again have a rifle strapped across her back. To be out with people she'd known since childhood, doing a task together they all knew was essential. And it was perhaps a moment of tactlessness on my part, but before I quite realized what I was saying I asked if she was afraid to die. I don't know if the question caught her off guard or if she just wanted to think for a while, to choose her words as carefully as possible, but we walked the rest of the way in silence, and it wasn't until we both had our coffees that she began to answer, tentatively at first: "I don't believe in dying. Don't believe there's anything good or glamorous or romantic about it. I believe in life. But there is another way in which when you're fighting for your life, and for the possibility for so many others to live more fully in the future, even if you might die, there's always something else there, where even your death has just as much to do with life as it does with loss. But don't get me wrong, that's definitely not what I want." She laughs and then suddenly we're both laughing. "I want to live as fully as possible."

I found her answer intense, intense in that way where maybe all you can do is laugh. I was still struggling with the death of my parents—something we never really get over but I now realize I was only just beginning to work my way through—when Zasulich came to stay with me, and in so many small intentional and unintentional ways she helped me through it. As the question of dying often hovered in and around the edges of our many conversations. And I saw, time and time again, that the reality that everyone dies was always, also, a question of how we should live. That to come fully to terms with our own impermanence was the only way one could begin to live for a cause larger than oneself. (In preparing to write this afterword I was often forced to reflect on how literature also has to do with the anxiety that one will die. To leave something behind and therefore disappear a little bit less completely.) I came to believe this might be one of the reasons our species wastes unprecedented amounts of time killing each other: we don't want to fully come to terms with the fact that we die so we try to hide from it—to gain the upper hand, so to speak—by taking the lives of others. If we are the bringer of death, how can we only be its victim? My parents died after having lived long and full lives, but if Zasulich were to, God forbid, die on patrol, she would be taken from us far too soon. And now she was my friend and already I was wishing she would stay with me forever.

When I more or less stopped being an artist, slowly, over time, all my old works disappeared or were destroyed. It is strange how painful I often still find it to think about this.

I had a storage space. When I moved here to look after my parents, many of the works I'd made over the course of my short life as an artist were stored there. And at one point I had to give it up, I couldn't afford it anymore. I emailed all my old friends, and the works were evenly distributed among them, people taking their favourites. But then, over the years, friends moved and moved again and it seems many of the works didn't manage to move with them. For obvious reasons, my old friends were often a bit embarrassed to provide exact details, so I'm not sure which works survived and which are now gone. But even at the beginning, when I first gave up the storage space, there were a few works that couldn't find a home and were left on the curb. (I unfortunately wasn't there, this was all negotiated long-distance.) Did I really imagine when I made those things that each and every one of them would last forever? Many of those works were made when I was quite young, and somehow when you're young you think (or hope) you might be immortal. And those were only works of art, not people or living things. Honestly, I was not some genius artist, it's no great loss. Though it can feel like one. I don't know if the lesson is that everything comes and goes and learning to live this is the only real form of sanity. That whatever we choose to fight for, it can't just be some shallow, puffed-up sense of permanence. The things we fight for have to be things that grow, evolve, and change. I suppose I could have had my old works shipped here, at great expense, and set them up in my parents' apartment, like a small museum dedicated to my former art practice. Then I could have found out if they would have survived the war. But for whatever reason, I chose not to. I chose to let go.

When I told Zasulich this story, she said she wished she

had one of my artworks now. She would take it with her. It would serve as something to remember me by. She asked me to describe these old works and I described as many as I could remember. I found it almost moving the way she listened to me describe things that once meant a great deal to me. If they no longer existed, at least they still existed in my memory and retelling of them, and the care and interest with which she listened allowed me to more fully feel this reality. It also made me question why she was so interested, and she explained that she grew up with little art but much talk of art, much desire for all the creativity everything they were working on would soon make possible. And people did at times use the metaphor of the experiment on the thin strip of land being almost like an artwork, in that it constantly involved ingenious solutions and leaps of faith. She told me the story of a meeting in which they were struggling with a practical problem—now she can no longer remember exactly what it was, that's obviously not the point of the story—and they'd hit a wall and were getting nowhere. Then someone said: "What if we were to look at this problem as an artwork?" And someone else said: "What could that possibly mean?" And they replied: "Let's look at it as an artwork. Let's not only propose concrete practical solutions. Let's propose any sort of solution our minds can fancy. Let's see what happens." And they did, people proposed every sort of crazy idea they could come up with. They still didn't come up with a solution, but it was more energizing and fun and she'd always remembered that meeting and admired the nerve it must have taken for whoever it was to propose that. "What if we were to look at the problem as an artwork?" You're at a serious meeting where everyone is frustrated and tense and then suddenly you open your mouth and say that. And what's more, everyone is open to it. They don't just tell you to shut up, but they're open to it and respond, give it a go. That very specific tone in her voice as she tells me: "We were all so open and alive then, the exact opposite of that university man who asked how he could be sure the society I was describing was as progressive and promising as I claimed." They didn't have to be sure because they were living it and making it so. And that in itself was a kind of art. And listening to me describe my long-gone works was in continuity with everything she was trying to explain to me. Because everything is connected.

Something that's true, and that I thought about the other day for the first time, is how Zasulich would never have ended up staying with me if it wasn't for this book. That's how we first met. She knew about "the friend" from the opening chapter, asked for my contact, and once we started corresponding, it seemed only natural that she'd stay with me on her way home. She contacted me as a friend of a friend. I hadn't read this book yet so knew nothing about her. But I did know about the struggle on the thin strip of land, and if she was returning there she had my full support. I so clearly remember meeting her at the airport. Due to the situation with oil, by that time there were already very few working cars. But the situation was relatively new so it was not yet clear how everything would or wouldn't work. I borrowed a friend's moped, it ran on electricity, you just plugged it into the wall, there weren't many of those around and energy shortages made them impractical. And halfway back to town the battery died and we had to walk, dragging her large suitcase behind us. Then the next day we had to walk back with a spare battery to retrieve the scooter. (On the walk back it crossed my mind a bicycle would have been better.) Those were the first long conversations we ever had. And yes, some of them were about the car accident and about our recently departed mutual friend. But I was amazed how quickly we found so many other things to speak about. When in my life had I found so much to talk about so quickly? The fact that there's so little access to cars now slows everything down. And, in a way, those first two conversations we had on those first two rather long walks, from and to the moped, were a product of this slowing down. And maybe that's how we first got in the habit of talking so much.

My life, during that time and since, wasn't only about Zasulich. One of the things that struck me about reading this book was the degree to which their liberation on the thin strip of land had to do with preparation, with the fact they had prepared, worked the soil, so to speak. That when the opportunity arose they were ready. I wanted to know if there was a way for me to do something similar. Build a foundation for an eventuality I was unable to predict. And I decided to start with children. Among ourselves we would often jokingly refer to it as the secret society, but there was nothing especially secret about it. There were definitely similarities to the community artworks I used to do before moving here, but I was careful never to frame it as art. It ended up being so simple. Children could stop by every Sunday afternoon and we'd talk about life and art. Sometimes we'd also act out stories from our lives and then try to change them in different ways, just to see what happens, what we can learn. At other times we'd act out stories we made up. When it got too large for me to do alone, I found a few friends and we split up into different rooms, often by age, but that part wasn't mandatory, every room filled with children laughing and talking. We encouraged listening, that was the main thing we worked on, how it was respectful to honestly listen when others spoke and it was reasonable to expect others to do the same for you. And there was also a fair bit of Socratic method, questioning things they said, things they'd heard from their parents or friends but had perhaps never heard anyone question before. The secret society part might have come in by making it clear that if they were too radical when speaking to their teachers, parents, or friends, there might be consequences. But it was less about being secretive and more about being careful. And even more about learning from each other. When Zasulich first came to stay with me, we all fit in two rooms, but by the time she left we were taking up almost four. Sometimes a worried parent would phone and I'd do my best to talk them down, asking them questions about what they'd heard, trying to get a quick snapshot of their beliefs, then framing it for them in ways I hoped they could accept. I didn't think what we were doing was so revolutionary. It was just a little experiment. I wasn't expecting results and had no real idea where it could lead.

While Zasulich was staying here she took over a room. She told me it was like the assemblies back on the thin strip of land, except with children instead of adults. She was so good at it, letting the children speak together, learn from each other, and then asking the right questions at exactly the right time. Watching her changed the way I approached the task. I saw that it could never be about providing the right idea, only about asking a productive question, that finding the thoughts for yourself was where the real pleasure lay, and it was often such pleasure that made the children more fully engage. I worried there would be trouble. That the authorities would catch wind of our experiment and shut it down. But so far we've managed to fly under the radar. The children really like the idea of a secret society, though most of them couldn't keep a secret to save their lives, and perhaps this game of mock secrecy is part of what allows it to continue. I'm not sure.

One morning at the café, Zasulich and I were talking about the secret-society children, as we often did, and she asked me what my hope was for them, for their future. Now it was my turn to take a long time to think. What I eventually said I'm still not sure I agree with. That we can never predict the future—the only thing we know for certain is it will never be quite how we imagine—so my hope is that these children will grow up to be honest and versatile enough to collectively manoeuvre their way through whatever may come, and that we've helped give them the tools to know they can't do it alone. But the reason I'm not sure I fully agree with this is I also know I hope for more. They are children of war and I hope they will use their experience to ensure such traumas don't endlessly repeat. But that is too much weight to put on their shoulders. And all we do on Sundays is meet and talk and play. I know, I tell myself, it is not nothing and at the same time wish I knew how to do more. Zasulich watches me after I've given my brief answer and can tell that something's up. It's not like she can read my mind, but she definitely knows me, it feels like she knows more than she could have possibly learned in the relatively brief time we've spent together. She says it's never useful to feel overly confident, but it's also not helpful underestimating one's efforts. Hope is most necessary when things are going badly, which is why we'll never run out. But not everything can go badly all the time, though frequently it might seem that way. She laughs as she says this, since what she wants to say is that she's certain so many of those children will remember our Sundays together for as long as they live, and sometimes such memories, when necessary, will give them the strength to fight. It means a lot to me that she says this. As she is doing so, I realize how I crave her approval. Like every (former) political artist, I long for a real revolutionary to tell me I've turned out okay. But I also know it's not really about that. She's just a friend giving me her full support. And she has the language and experiences to do so. And I believe, if one day I fuck up, she would also tell me. And I hope, if she did so, that I might have the capacity and strength to fully listen and then change my ways.

There was something else I tried to edge toward with the children, I believe it might have had to do with shame. If one of the children made a comment and other children teased them for it, I would never let it pass unnoticed. When I was younger I honestly didn't realize how powerful shame was, how often it shapes our decisions and actions. I read once that, as children, our personalities are shaped more by our peers, by other children, than by our parents or other adults. This continues to feel true to me, and it's an idea that's never far from my thoughts every single Sunday afternoon. When a child is teased, to always raise the possibility that whatever they might have said is nothing to be ashamed of. And that thinking or speaking in the moment never means we are tied to it forever.

For several weeks now I've been asking myself how I should end this afterword. An obvious ending might be Zasulich's departure, though that is actually no ending at all since both our lives have continued and we often correspond. In one recent letter, Zasulich wrote about how strange it was to be home. Everything was exactly how she remembered and everything was completely different. Things felt easier and harder at the same time: the present more established, the future more uncertain. She was telling everyone about me and hoping I someday wanted to visit. With so few working cars it was considerably more difficult to get there, but she was sure we could find a way. The lack of oil was proving challenging on so many levels but also felt like the challenge they had been waiting for their entire lives. How to do so many things in the most ecological ways they could imagine. Unfortunately warplanes appeared to have more than enough fuel. When there's a shortage you really learn what people's priorities are, and it seems, for many governments, dropping bombs remained near the top of the list. But nothing essential had been bombed yet. She looked forward to a day when the planes would run out of oil. That would really be cause to rejoice. But, not to be cynical, before rejoicing ceased she was certain solar warplanes wouldn't be far behind.

So many of her old friends were telling her she had changed, that her time away had changed her, but she didn't feel she had changed. Nonetheless, she often tried to understand how she might have changed, what exactly they were trying to tell her. Before she left she'd spent her entire life on the thin strip of land. But while she was away she had travelled constantly, giving workshops, presentations, and talks. A sedentary life temporarily replaced by a nomadic one, and now that she's back, all that moving about feels almost like a dream. How had that dream, which was clearly also real, changed her? It was as if she now had a more concrete understanding of what they were up against—not just the physical dangers that directly surrounded them but also a whole series of perspectives, a way of thinking about life and value, that had consumed so much of the world. Now that she was back, it forced her to fully consider and articulate her own values. She wrote that the only values she was able to care about were values in connection with those who surrounded her. That even if they didn't agree about everything, their values were still in connection, their differences were being developed together. So in a way she never wants to completely know what her own values are. She only wants to feel them in and out of connection with those who surround her, as an ongoing process of negotiation. And since this is something that most fully occurs on the thin strip of land, even though she is grateful she's had the chance to see a bit of the world and spread the word about their cause, she hopes she will not leave again.

I remember the feeling I had when I finished reading that particular letter, which was only one of many we've exchanged. A feeling that our lives were so different, and yet when I came back here to look after my parents, perhaps it was also a tentative first step toward finding a sense of place. I certainly don't think it needs to be about going back to where you're from, only about a sense of commitment to a specific situation and a hope to see it improve over time. To feel it improve into the future, over many lifetimes, many generations. I remember when the author of this book was staying with me—a few days before he left like a thief in the night to so stupidly walk through the war—and I thought: Is it really so simple, that I'm an optimist and he's a pessimist, that I see potential almost everywhere while he often sees little or none, that the state of the world brutally fuels his depression to the point of despair while I am generally able to see it all as a question of what I might next do to help, even if it only means helping one or a few people? But I don't know if it's that simple. Even in his despair he managed to do a few small things and even in my hope I have sometimes managed to do nothing.

He was one kind of friend, from my past, and Zasulich is a different kind of friend, from my present, and I can even see the three of us on a kind of spectrum, from least effective to most, where I'm in the middle, and, with friends on each side, it feels like the middle is exactly the right place to be. But not for everyone. As Zasulich just said, the value of our thoughts and actions is in connection. In this particular analogy, to be clear, I like the middle because there are friends on both sides. And because the dead are still with us. In our memories of them and in what they said and wrote and left behind. And perhaps in other ways as well.

I will also tell you about the day Zasulich left, since it was certainly a significant day in my life. I knew she wasn't staying forever. I knew she was just staying for a few months on her way home. But nonetheless, it's strange how the closer she got to leaving, the more I hoped she would stay. It's strange how knowing someone a few months can feel like you've known them several lifetimes. I asked myself: If she was leaving to go somewhere safer, would it still bother me as much? Because I wanted her to stay, but more than that I was worried for her life. I'm not sure how justified such fears were. Was it really any more dangerous on the thin strip of land than it was here or anywhere else? As the saying goes, you could be hit by a car tomorrow. But what they were fighting for was so important and therefore I couldn't help but fear that those who wanted it stamped out would fight against them even harder. A positive example can serve as an example for the world, and so those who want the world to remain the way it is do their best not to allow any. (Which is also why we're constantly being told that what occurs on the thin strip of land isn't possible.) It wasn't simply the struggle on the thin strip of land. It was Zasulich. Why would I care more that she dies than if any of her comrades died? There is no political reason, only a personal one. Yes, it would bother me more if Zasulich was harmed than if

Goldman, Huerta, or Zana was harmed. Because Zasulich is now my friend and the others are just names in a book. Should I then ask myself if this is also part of the problem, that those who are close feel more precious than those who are far away? I feel both things need to be true. We need to care where we care most and also struggle to make such care wider, as wide as possible. But the reality of our immediate attachments should not be understated.

It was a bright summer day. I knew the day was coming but I'd lost track of exactly when, didn't realize it was now. I came into the living room and she was packing. She had arrived with one suitcase and was leaving the same way. I must have looked like I was seeing a ghost because she immediately stopped what she was doing, came over, and gave me a long, full hug. She held me for a while and then, more or less in silence, I helped her finish packing. We walked through the apartment one last time to check if she'd left anything behind. Walking from room to room felt a bit like a ritual. It crossed my mind to ask her to stay, but I knew that would be selfish. She knew what she needed to do, where she belonged, and I knew it even more so. Perhaps there was also a possibility I could have gone with her, but it didn't cross my mind. There was nothing left to do but say goodbye. As we were doing so, I thought about how long it had been since I'd made a new friend, a real one. It occurred to me that Zasulich was the first new friend in quite a long time. And realizing this, I suddenly knew it wasn't over, I would be more open with people in the years to come. In saying goodbye to Zasulich, I also promised myself I would care more for the friends I had and there would also someday be a few more. And then we said good-bye, and we were both crying, then we were both laughing, and then she was gone.

It's taken a lot out of me, writing this afterword. So many emotions, memories, and questions. Politics and life. What to put in and what to leave out. If I'm to have the final word, I thought I should try to make it count. Say what felt to me most important. But there is no such thing as the final word. I remember that feeling right after she left. Sitting in my parents' apartment, now my apartment, which in some sense also belongs to the Sunday-afternoon children, and which at that precise moment felt so utterly empty. Thinking about Zasulich and the long journey she has ahead of her before finally arriving home. Telling myself she will survive—not just the journey but far into the future. Telling myself I will see her again. Hopefully it won't be too long.

Note

This book was, at its very beginning, inspired by the three cantons of Rojava (also known as the Autonomous Administration of North and East Syria, or Western Kurdistan). It was inspired by Rojava while, at the same time, I felt I had no right to directly take on that subject. I, of course, even question myself—much as I question myself about so many things—about the extent to which I have the right to be inspired by it. But I was inspired, as we all should be.

And then, as I wrote, other revolutionary moments informed my conscious and unconscious thoughts: first and foremost Rojava (2012–), but then also: the Spanish Revolution (1936), the Sandinistas (1961–), the Zapatistas (1994–), and the Argentinian Neighbourhood Assembly Movement (2001–03). It is obvious that my knowledge about each of these movements and their cultural contexts is far from complete.

Coming back to the essential importance of Rojava to this book, I should now specify some aspects of life on the "thin strip of land" that are more directly inspired by Rojava's ongoing revolutionary struggles: the former government withdrawing from the area due to the civil war and the region declaring autonomy (this was unique to the situation in that region of Syria); the horizontal decision-making and participatory democracy that are key elements of Abdullah Öcalan's[1] ideology; the feminism and eco-socialism (also major tenets of Abdullah Öcalan's ideology); the locals calling their community "the experiment" (a term often used in the documentaries and articles about Rojava); the majority of fighters being female and the emphasis on female fighters in general (the heaviest coverage in mainstream media of Rojava has been of its female units fighting ISIS). These resonances, and others like them, weren't always intentional as I was writing. I considered pulling back, because I was worried this book was too much about Rojava in ways I continue to question. But I now believe it is better to leave these resonances in, hopefully inspiring readers to learn more about this reality in the future. (Since this book is not reality.)

May the bravery and insights of their struggle inform our future bravery and struggles and may we continue to learn from their mistakes. There is much to read, and much that continues to be written, past and present, and I would hope this book might be one reflection within a larger network of writings, actions, and thoughts.

---

[1] Abdullah Öcalan is a key thinker and founding member of the Kurdistan Workers' Party. Since 1999 he has been a political prisoner in İmralı prison in the Sea of Marmara (Turkey).

Acknowledgements

I would deeply like to thank all those who read—or in other ways helped me think about—this book during various states of its incompletion. Your insights and questions were invaluable for my ongoing understanding of what I was working on. Infinite thanks to: Mirna Boyadjian, Mojeanne Behzadi, Erin Brubacher, Heman Chong, Alexei Perry Cox, Jeremy M. Davies, Adriana Disman, Burcu Emeç, Danica Evering, Eunsong Kim, Adam Kinner, Joni Murphy, Nayla Naoufal, Eva Neklyaeva, Ted Rutland, and Christopher Willes.

It would have been impossible for me to complete this book without the generous support of a writing residency at the Santarcangelo Festival, where I spent a few weeks in March 2019 trying to come up with some sort of ending. I am grateful for their hospitality and support.

I also wish to acknowledge the support of the Canada Council for the Arts and the Conseil des arts et des lettres du Québec, without which the writing of this book would have also simply not been possible.

About the Author

JACOB WREN makes literature, performances, and exhibitions. His books include *Revenge Fantasies of the Politically Dispossessed*, *Polyamorous Love Song* (finalist for the Fence Modern Prize in Prose and a *Globe and Mail* best book of 2014), *Rich and Poor* (finalist for the Paragraphe Hugh MacLennan Prize for Fiction and a *Globe and Mail* best book of 2016), and *Authenticity Is a Feeling*. He is artistic co-director of the Montreal-based interdisciplinary group PME-ART. Wren lives in Montreal.

Colophon

Manufactured as the first edition of
Dry Your Tears to Perfect Your Aim
in the fall of 2024 by Book*hug Press

Edited for the press by Malcolm Sutton
Copy-edited by Stuart Ross
Proofread by Laurie Siblock
Type + design by Malcolm Sutton
Cover image: Kim Kölle Valentine. Used with permission.

Printed in Canada

bookhugpress.ca